THAT SINKING FEELING

THAT SINKING FEELING

JANYRE TROMP

That Sinking Feeling

Published by Kregel Publications, a division of Kregel, Inc., P.O. Box 2607, Grand Rapids, MI 49501.

ISBN 0-8254-3887-X

Printed in the United States of America

06 07 08 09 10 / 5 4 3 2 1

THAT SINKING FEELING

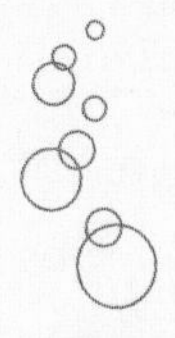

Chapter 1

The water shimmered in the bright sunlight. The aqua blue expanse before us was warm and clean, and definitely not Lake Michigan. It was just the two of us, Max and me, standing in a small, flat-bottomed Whaler rigged with a special dive exit and ladder on the side of the boat.

Tied to a pole above the awning, a small red flag with a diagonal white stripe snapped in the wind. Max and I stood together in our black dive gear at the side of the boat, our arms touching. A wisp of hair escaped my loose braid and twisted across my face, playing in the wind. With a slight nod of my head, we took a giant stride off the boat and splashed into the ocean.

My body slipped below the surface in a stream of white bubbles. Then we were descending through the unbelievably aqua water, looking up at the bottom of the boat as it rocked slowly in the water. Freedom.

Color flickered everywhere. Corals of red, yellow, and blue stuck up out of the rock. Huge hollow tubes, tiny wavy arms. I was seeing things I'd only seen in pictures at my dad's dive shop. This was nothing like my dives in the lakes around home.

A school of round, pancake-thin fish streaked by—a stream of purple in the blue. I reached out my hand to touch them, and they darted away from me.

I turned to point them out to Max but couldn't find him. I spread my fins wide to stop my forward motion and hovered for a moment, looking to both sides, above, and below. There was no sign of my best friend. I checked again, looking for his black, silky hair floating above him, his neon yellow tank, or his blue swim fin peeking out from behind the reef wall. Nothing. The sun slashed the surface of the water, turning my breath into tiny shimmering bubbles rushing to the surface for escape.

I was going to kill him when I found him. He was not supposed to take off without letting his dive buddy know what was going on. I waited, watching.

The colors swirled. A jagged edge of rock; a silver barracuda, its teeth bared; a mammoth red snapper prowling. I swallowed, pushing my long hair out of the way of my mask. Looking down at my dive computer, I started the prescribed countdown before I would surface to find my buddy.

It had already occurred to me that it wasn't like Max to pull a prank like this. When I looked at my computer, I realized my hands were shaking. I forced myself to slow my breathing. *Breathe. Just breathe.*

Something grabbed my shoulder and I jumped. "Max!"

But it wasn't Max. My dad stood over me, shaking me gently. "Audrey, wake up. If you want to come to the shop with me, I'll take you and Max out diving after I finish setting up today's training dives."

I merely nodded and rubbed my eyes, trying to get rid of the shaky feeling in my stomach. I hate nightmares. My dad smiled and ruffled my hair.

"You've got thirty minutes. Better get moving."

I blinked, shoved back the covers, and sat on the edge of my bed. I knew it had been just a dream, but I couldn't completely convince myself that everything was okay. The images in my head were real enough to be those of some premonition-spouting wacko, but it was only a late-night-snack-induced nightmare.

I watched my dad as he continued talking about the plans for the day—where we'd dive, what we'd do. He always knew when I needed him to stay with me. I watched him pick up my clothes from the day before and toss them expertly into the hamper in my closet. He continued until my heartbeat returned to normal and I could almost forget the image of a limp, broken Max. With a lopsided smile, he walked to the hallway and around the corner.

People have told me that I look like my dad, but I've never thought so. He is what everyone calls handsome, and I'd say I'm just on the wrong side of cute. I have his long legs, dark wavy hair, and sparkly blue eyes. But on me, the legs are gangly and always in the way, my hair is constantly out of control, my nose is slightly too large . . . well, you get the idea.

My older brother, Ben, always told me that he'd had to grow into dad's features, and that I would, too. Which is great, but I don't ever remember a time when Ben didn't have girls draped all over him.

One thing the three of us—Dad, Ben, and me—definitely have in common is a love of the water. I suppose I'm a bit spoiled for a broke thirteen-year-old water-lover. Not only do I reside in Michigan—known for its amazing white, sandy beaches and water in endless supply—but my folks own a dive shop, which means we make our living in, on, and around the water.

To this day I still can't figure out what made my mom want the dive shop. She's always seemed the opposite of Dad. Precise, neat to the point of obsession, and absolutely in love with the "safe thing." My dad has told us that Mom once loved diving. But I don't remember that. Ben says he can't remember our mom so much as swimming when we were little, let alone struggling into dive gear and risking the depths.

I remember that before he went down to Kalamazoo for college, Ben would try to get my mom to go with us to the beach. But Mom would always decline, and instead would take my fluffy little sister, Suzie, to tea or to the art museum. Ben and I used to joke that she didn't dive because of how unclean it was to dive in gear that couldn't really be washed.

The smell of pancakes cooking on the griddle finally lured me out of bed, and I shuffled as quickly as I could to the bathroom. I didn't do too badly for a sleep-numbed, summer-vacationing thirteen-year-old. I successfully avoided my little sister (my mom's annoying double in miniature), ate a yummy pancake breakfast without syrup landing in my lap, and managed to scramble through the back door as my dad opened it to leave.

Dad had apparently called Max's mom while I was in the shower, because when we arrived at the shop, Max was there with a bag, looking as if he was ready to dive at that very moment.

Even though I knew the images in my head were from a dream, it was good to see my friend alive and well. I jumped out of the car and waved. He waved back, crinkling his stubby nose at me, his black hair looking almost blue in the bright sunlight. He was laughing at me . . . likely a response to my soaking wet hair and more than usually wrinkled T-shirt and jean shorts.

"Just fill the tanks and I'll be back soon," Dad was saying to me as he walked away to greet a group of adults clustered around the dive shop's truck and boat.

"Bummer." A great way to summarize the task of filling the aluminum cylinders that provided air to divers.

Chapter 2

"Yeow!" I stood, shaking out the pain in my fingers. It was the third time I'd smashed my fingers between a scuba tank and the cooling basin.

Max calmly took the tank and put it next to the others that had been filled. He wiped his wet hands on the back of his otherwise spotless khaki shorts, his dark, almond-shaped eyes glittering. "Audrey, if you'd go slower, it might help."

"Yeah, yeah. I think it's time *you* tried pulling these things in and out of here." I yanked another one out of the basin where it had stood while I pumped compressed air into it. "My arms feel like Jell-O, and these tanks weigh five hundred pounds apiece." The bottle clanged loudly against the floor in agreement.

"More like thirty." He always had to be precise. "Your dad'll be back from the training dives any minute."

He didn't have to add that he wasn't allowed to mess with the compressor. It wasn't one of those parental "because I said so" rules, either. The compressor really was dangerous, and if I wasn't careful about how fast I filled one of the aluminum containers and how much air I pumped in, things could get ugly fast.

I guess it really didn't matter. I hadn't been serious about Max pulling tanks anyway. I never had him over to the shop to work—I just liked his company.

Max would always stand in the corner by the door cracking jokes, pushing his smooth, slightly curly hair out of his eyes. If you just looked at us, you'd say we were exact opposites. There were the obvious things. He's Cambodian from his mom and German from his dad. But he looks completely Cambodian—jet-black hair; a smallish, rather pointed nose; and small, almost black eyes.

He's tall and lean (which comes from his dad), always neat and clean, and put together (which comes from his mom).

I'm just a mutt and not ever quite as presentable as Max. That's how it's always been with us.

Even after we'd play soccer or bike through the neighborhood, I'd always manage to be the one with hair spiked at crazy angles, grass stains and grease adorning me somewhere. It was almost like I was his stain shield or something. All the dirt that should have landed on him ended up on me instead.

Despite our differences, we've always been the best of friends. He knows more about me than just about anyone. He knows how much I love the freedom I find in the water. And he knows how much I always try to be what my mom wants me to be.

On the other hand, I know how much Max loves soccer. I know he's a good friend, despite being a year older than I am. And I know just how much it hurt Max to have his father walk out on him, his mom, and his brother.

We never have to say much to know what the other is thinking.

If anything like this morning's dream ever were to come true. . . . I pushed the thought from my head as soon as it started forming. I didn't need to know what I would do without him around. He'd always be there for me.

I grinned at him. Hauling another cylinder out of the washtub, my muscles strained until I thought I'd pass out. "Here, at least put this over there for me." I jerked my head to the left, pointing to where the other filled tanks stood. I wasn't trying to be lazy or anything. I'd been in the little wood-paneled room for about thirty-five minutes, lifting tanks in and out of the tub over and over and over again. I knew I was strong for a thirteen-year-old, especially for a girl, but my arms were getting tired.

Max took my burden and hefted it with relative ease. "Wimp."

I stuck out my tongue and pulled out another tank. My tight grip on the yoke slipped, twisting the black knob and opening the air valve. The hiss of escaping air made me jump and drop the tank. Everyone in my dad's dive shop swiveled, staring back into the corner room where we stood rigid. I felt my cheeks turn red and suddenly I was in motion—cranking the valve closed, flinging the tank to the opposite side of the room, and slamming the door shut.

Max let out a huge, rumbling laugh, the kind that is so hard and long, it rams your eyes closed and forces you to the nearest wall for support, 'cause you're shaking so hard. I let out a reluctant little giggle, which made him stop abruptly and look up at me with his lips pinched together; then he laughed even harder. At some point he slouched over, gripping his sides, gasping for air as he laughed at me. I didn't think it was *that* funny.

Indignant, I stormed out the door, grabbed an empty tank from around the corner, and swung it over the edge of the tub. It slipped in with a splash that soaked me from my head to my waist. Water dripped from the tip of my nose. You'd have thought I was the funniest comedian in the world, the way he was carrying on. Frankly, I hated having a wet T-shirt—a spectacle made worse by the bathing suit I wore underneath—and wasn't thrilled with my best friend laughing at me. But I knew I looked ridiculous. I started into a well-practiced eye roll when Max's inhale suddenly turned into a series of snorts. I broke. In two seconds flat *I* was slumped against the door, laughing uncontrollably.

We were still trying to control ourselves enough to finish filling the scuba tanks for my dad when I heard the sound of a truck pulling up to the garage door out back. It was what we'd been waiting for all morning.

"He's back!"

"Yep. And you've still got three tanks to fill."

That time I completed the eye roll and quickly followed it with a full tongue thrust. But I decided not to argue. I dumped the other tanks into the water, attached the fill valves, and turned on the air.

Slowly the pin in the gauge moved up as the compressor behind the wood-paneled wall revved up to push more air through the lines. I pushed my way-too-long bangs out of my eyes and tapped my stubby fingernails on the washtub. I could hear my mom in the back of my mind: "You need a haircut, Audrey. Someone's going to think you've been out to sea for two years."

If she would just let me cut it all off, it wouldn't be a problem. But soon it'd all be tucked inside a dive hood and out of my way anyway. Dad was back from the training dives, and he was going to take Max and me diving. Dad was one of only a few certified adults Mom allowed me down with, and he was almost always too busy with the store to dive with us. So, we'd had little "bottom time," and summer break was already half over.

The red signal light flashed on, jerking me out of my thoughts. The little pin on the gauge read 3,000 psi. "Finally," I said with a sigh. Spinning the valve to the compressor closed, I yanked the inlets off the T-shaped yokes on the top of each tank and put the lines back on the hooks anchored into the wall.

Just as I was bending my knees and starting to lift a tank out of the water, I heard a deep "Hey, pumkin'" behind me, and a wad of paper smacked me between the shoulders, making me jump.

I dropped the tank and whirled around. It was Dad, as I always pictured him in my mind—leaning against the doorframe grinning, eyes shining, his dark hair slightly damp and tousled from being in the water. Even though I'd never admit it to another living soul, I loved it when Dad called me "pumkin'." It always made me feel like I was still his little girl. I started a smile but caught myself, grimacing for Max's benefit—Max counted as another living soul. I turned back to my work with a quick "Hey," and braced myself to wrestle another scuba tank out of the tub.

"Here, let me get those for you." In half a second, Dad grabbed a tank in each hand and whipped them out of the water as if they were just gigantic marshmallows (rather than aluminum containers weighing thirty pounds apiece). When he set them on the floor, I noticed there wasn't a drop of water on him. I saw him looking at my not-so-dry T-shirt, hair that was everywhere despite the ponytail holder, and my grubby jean shorts. He lifted his eyebrows, making two little lines appear between them, and shook his head.

"That's my girl."

It was a statement of pride, not annoyance. Not only was my dad an ally against my "Here, put on this lovely lacey thing" mom, his blue-gray eyes always flickered with the adventure that was guaranteed when you were around him.

"If you'll fill the tanks from the divers coming in, I'll check and make sure Jason and Janine have the counter under control. When you're finished, load up your gear and we'll go dive."

Great, more tanks. I backhanded Max's arm for the snicker he wasn't hiding too well, but traded my own groan for a grin reflecting my dad's excitement. We were going to go dive, and despite my weird dream, diving's all that mattered that afternoon.

Max, who seemed to be able to handle the tanks better than I, grabbed a few of the empty tanks from the hallway and dropped them into the water for me. I got to work, hooking everything up and filling the tanks for Dad's waiting customers.

Since the diving community is pretty small, I knew most of the divers and said a quick hello to them all. There was a new guy talking animatedly with Mr. Broome, my dad's favorite among the scuba instructors on his roster. As I pulled the last tank out of the water, the new arrival burst into a surprisingly high-pitched laugh for a guy of his burly size. Max and I exchanged looks. Mr. Broome was a nice guy, but he certainly wasn't *that* funny. Like most instructors, he had a "real job," too—he was a lawyer of some sort. Shrugging, I carried Mr. Broome's tank over to him and set it down.

"Thanks, Audrey." Mr. Broome grinned down at me, his eyes sparkling beneath bushy eyebrows.

Mr. Broome was one of the most relaxed and capable people I knew. He was not a giant of a man, nor had he ever been a military leader—he just projected that sort of image. In reality he probably was a hair over five-nine. His straight posture and razor-sharp diction were due to his life in boarding school while his parents were missionaries in South America.

Trying not to get in the way, I turned to go gather my gear. But the new guy stepped right into my path, nearly running over me. He pranced to the back door without acknowledging me, and literally tripped out into the bright sunshine.

Once the guy was out of sight, Mr. Broome pushed his drying hair away from his face and mopped the newbie's wet footprints off the floor. "Nice guy." Mr. Broome shook his head at what had just taken place.

Mr. Broome folded himself into a chair behind the counter and looked up at me. "Going diving with your dad?"

I couldn't help smiling. Going diving was almost worth the wait and slave labor. "Yep. We're diving the wreck out front." An unnamed tugboat wreck was across the street and down the shore a little ways from the shop. Lying at a depth of about fifty feet, the tug rested just in front of a deep-blue expanse of water—a huge drop-off. It was one of my favorite shore dives—it was easy, but a lot of fish hovered beneath the protection of the drowned boat.

"You'll love it today. The water's gorgeous and my dives were great despite the company. I'd go out with you guys, but I'm flying out tomorrow night and I'm already pushing the deco limits."

In diver lingo, "pushing the deco limits" means risking getting "bent"—a painful, potentially deadly diver illness. While the limits, a combination of time and depth charts, were meant to keep divers safe, they also got in the way of every diver's bottom time.

It was always when I was finning toward a huge fish or some obscure object I'd seen out of the corner of my eye, that my dad pointed to his gauge and then jerked a thumbs-up—time to return to the surface. I'm too young to be trained in decompression diving, but I dreamed of the day I could stay down longer. Mr. Broome was definitely a fellow water-lover who sometimes pushed the edges of safety for another opportunity to get wet.

Despite the annoyance, I never disobeyed the limits. I still don't completely understand how it all works, but it has something to do with the pressure of the water making you breathe in a greater amount of nitrogen. The longer you stay down or the deeper you go, the more nitrogen there is in your body. So, if you were to come up too fast or stay down too long, you risked little bubbles of nitrogen developing in your body. I'm no doctor, but I know a nitrogen bubble in my brain is not a desirable thing.

But at least for today the limits wouldn't be a problem. We'd only have time for one dive before Dad needed to be back at the shop to give the person on the night shift a break for dinner.

Mr. Broome checked with the divers to be sure they had everything, and then strode out to the parking lot with his tank and gear bag trailing little drips of water behind him.

I turned back to the compressor room to see Max stuffing his blue-and-black wet suit into his gear bag.

"How do you get that thing into your bag? I can't ever get my bag zipped with that mammoth suit in there."

"Dunno. Your bag's already packed, though." He paused just a second, then added, "Wetsuit and all." His black eyes twinkled at me. I knew he was just trying to get a rise out of me because he could do something I couldn't, so I smiled my happy smile to let him know I was on to him. I didn't think he could get the corners of his mouth up any higher. But he did, just to show me up. And I loved him for it. Max was the best friend anyone could ever have. A pain sometimes, but a good guy anyway.

"Let's go dive, my friend." He grabbed my arm and wheeled me around the corner—right into my dad.

We both grinned up at my dad for a split second before the look in his eyes deep-sixed our excitement.

"Sorry, guys. No diving tonight. Janine didn't show up for her shift, so I need to stay here and cover for her."

"Can't Jason stay a little longer to cover?"

"Audrey." The way he said it—half sigh, half frustrated exclamation—made me snap my mouth closed. It also helped that Max put a well-placed elbow into my gut, but I wouldn't have said anything if I could have, and that's the point.

My dad took a deep breath and let it out slowly. His eyes had lost that sparkle I loved. No adventure for today. Max rescued the moment before I could think of anything "helpful" to say.

"Don't worry about it, Mr. Barringer. Some other time. Come on, Audrey." We walked slowly past the counter. It felt like a funeral march.

This was the fourth time in two weeks that Janine hadn't shown up for work. Dad was going to have to fire her. Nothing else would explain the look in my dad's eyes. It also meant we weren't likely to go diving until Dad could find a replacement for the store. Our main Mom-approved dive partner was out of commission for who knew how long.

Chapter 3

Outside, I plopped down on a cement curb in the parking lot, the asphalt warm through my once white canvas shoes.

Staring down at the ground, I watched ants scurry around the edge of the asphalt, being productive. My brain whirred, wondering what we were going to do for fun the rest of August. Suddenly, summer vacation seemed like it would drag into eternity—destined to be one of the worst in recent memory.

A deep voice broke up my pity party. "Too bad I can't take you guys with me." It was Mr. Broome. He closed the trunk of his little red sports car and turned toward us.

"Where you going this time, Mr. Broome?" Mr. Broome was Max's hero. He had traveled all over the world, often the first American to dive some site only the locals had seen. His stories and gorgeous underwater photos of remote areas were a couple of the things that helped Max get over his fear of drowning and be trained to dive.

"I'm actually going to Cambodia."

"Seriously?! That's where my mom's from."

"Yeah, I know. I've even learned some Khmer so that the team won't be completely lost when we're over there. At least I know how to ask for a bathroom or the American embassy."

"Jum-reap soo-a." I jerked around toward Max. I had no idea what he'd just said, but it was definitely something not in English.

"Tau neak sok sapbaiy jea teh?" answered Mr. Broome. My attention snapped back to Mr. Broome.

A ringing came from Mr. Broome's side before I could comment on the rudeness of excluding me by speaking some secret language.

"Sohm dtoh," Mr. Broome said as he turned to answer his phone. He listened for a moment with a few "uh-huhs," then glanced at us and smiled apologetically before walking to his car. Just before starting the car he hung up, pulled on his maroon Western Michigan baseball cap, and drove away.

"What was that?" I hadn't really meant to yell at Max, but from his expression, I had.

"It's Khmer." At my blank look he explained that Khmer is the most common language spoken in Cambodia, as if that explained anything.

Max's raised eyebrow made me realize that my mouth was hanging open like my neighbor's drooly Saint Bernard. I snapped it shut. I had no idea Max could speak two languages. I had thought his mom had pretty much severed ties with the country that had killed her uncle and nearly killed her and her mom. Bizarre.

"Well, now what?"

"What?" He'd lost me.

"We were trying to figure out what we were gonna do. Remember?"

"Oh, yeah." I was having trouble processing at the moment. My brain was still stuck on the revelations of the past two minutes: (a) Mr. Broome could get a semi-functional grasp of a very foreign language in what must have been a very short period of time; and (b) Max spoke Khmer. He'd been my best friend since I was eight and he was nine, and I didn't know he could speak his mom's language. . . . I could barely say the name of the language, let alone wrap my tongue around the rest of it.

Max blew out a breath and rolled his eyes at my unusual silence.

"My grandma taught it to me. Despite the fact that everything Cambodian freaks my mom out, Grandma didn't want me to lose my Cambodian heritage. And since she didn't speak English all that well, it was the only way we could communicate when she babysat Shawn and me."

I knew that Max and his older brother, Shawn, had spent a lot of time with Mrs. Myer's mom after Mr. Myer left, and I also knew that Mr. Myer had left when Max was quite little. But I hadn't met Max's grandma before she died, so I guess I'd never put it all together.

"Hello? Earth to Audrey."

"Um? Oh, yeah. I guess we could walk over to the dive site across the street. Maybe someone will be there who can take us down."

It was moments like these that I missed my older brother, Ben. He would have been able to talk Dad into letting us go. But that was one area in which Ben and I were totally different. I couldn't sweet-talk anyone.

Since we weren't going far, we left our bikes between the fence slats. They weren't likely to be stolen. Even if our bikes were fancy or new, and they weren't, the handlebars barely stuck above the evergreen bushes underneath the sign that read "Blue-Water Dive Shop" in huge, faded red letters.

We trotted across the street and up the little hill on the other side. We looked down to our left. The white sand shimmered in the sunshine. To the right, the beach, dotted with homes, curved around the bay and disappeared in the rippling water of the lake in the distance. No one.

But I trotted down the backside of the hill anyway, kicking at the tufts of beach grass on the way down.

Turning left, I walked down to the edge of the bay, Max trudging beside me.

Normally he would have argued the futility of walking down the beach, as it was obvious to anyone with eyes that there was no one available to talk to or dive with; but he didn't.

I suppose he realized that we both were condemned to spend the rest of the day wandering around with nothing to do. We might as well start it without an argument.

We continued to follow the curve of the water, which was as still and as clear as the cold waters of Lake Michigan ever got—perfect for diving.

I took off my shoes and splashed forward in the water to avoid a little outcropping of trees and shrubs. I was incredibly allergic to just about every wildflower and weed that grew in the woods of Northern Michigan. Max just grinned and began weaving through the little trees.

Concentrating on the water spreading to my right and squishing my toes into the white sand, I missed Max's full facial plant into the ground. But I heard the crash and subsequent sputtering.

"You okay?" I scrambled out of the water, ignoring the pricking sticks at the edge of the tree line.

Max's head popped out of the undergrowth, complete with a maple leaf sticking feather-like out of the back of his normally smooth black hair. I pinched my lips together, trying not to laugh.

He grinned at me, daring me to laugh. I just offered my hand to help him up.

"What happened?"

"I tripped."

"Yeah. That was obvious. Over what?"

He turned and picked up a yellow boat-mooring line. One side had a knot in it, and that was stuck between a rock and a tree stump. The other was connected to one of those big, black, airtight drums.

It was kind of like the ones people fill with cement and drop to the bottom of inland lakes to hold a buoy in place.

Max pulled the drum out from under the brush a little bit. I carefully stepped around the spiky weeds at the edge of the woods, moving in to investigate with him. We were always up for a good mystery, especially considering our options for the day.

The lid was held down by only one of the four clamps attached to the top. But when we pushed the lid off and peered inside, the drum was empty. So much for that investigation.

Stepping back out of the trees, I stepped directly onto a sharp object.

It was *my* turn to end up in an ungraceful heap on the ground. I could only manage a whimper as I pulled my injured foot up to examine it. Something had sliced my heel in a clean, straight line. Fortunately, I have tough heels, and although the injury produced quite a bit of blood, it could have been worse.

Max squatted down next to me and yanked my foot around toward him.

"Ouch! Are you trying to kill me?" I'd barely regained my balance from having been jerked around, when he unceremoniously dropped my foot and began rummaging in the leaves and underbrush. I was still in the process of forming a wonderful statement about his rudeness, when he nodded his head and made a little whistling sound.

"Yep. I thought so." He took off his shirt.

"Thought what? What are you doing?" A sliced foot was no call for stripping down in the forest.

Using his shirt as a handkerchief, he reached forward and gingerly picked something up off the forest floor. "That cut was too clean and straight to be from a stick." He'd switched into Sherlock Holmes mode. I was pretty sure he'd gotten it from his mom, who'd turned all her energy into righting the wrongs of the world as an investigative reporter.

"And look, it's got a weird symbol on it."

He finally handed me the cause of my despair, still grasping the object with his T-shirt. It was one of those multipurpose Swiss Army-type knives. I clicked the blade shut and flipped the knife over in my hand.

I swallowed hard. It bore a mark similar to one I'd seen elsewhere. And if it was the same, we'd stumbled onto major crime evidence.

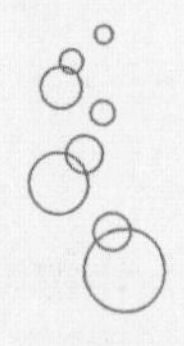

Chapter 4

I traced the mark with my finger, studying the image of a woman with a long, vaguely oriental face and wearing a hat made of stacked rings in the shape of a pyramid.

"Don't touch it, Audrey! There could be fingerprints on it." Max snatched the knife back with his shirt.

"Wow. You'd think I was trying to kill someone." But he was right, of course.

Mrs. Myer had been assigned to investigate a rash of lakeshore burglaries that had occurred over the past few months for the local paper. The police suspected the robbers used a boat for their transportation to and from their victims' homes, because each home was on the water and neighbors consistently said they'd heard a loud boat motor before, and sometimes after, the burglaries. Since the robberies had occurred at night during low-speed "no wake" hours, revving boat engines stuck out. The only other clue the police had discovered was the image of the woman with the funky hat carved into a doorpost at every crime scene.

It looked like we may have found a clue. Max started digging frantically through the underbrush—Sherlock Holmes mode again. He slid the black barrel slightly forward and stooped to look at the ground. He stood quickly, snatched one of my socks out of my hand, and knelt down to pick up a black leather case, just a bit longer and wider than a pencil case.

Frowning, Max carefully unzipped the case and pulled out a thin metal tool. It was a rod, about as big around as my pinky, with a thin hook on one end.

"What are dental tools doing out here?" I asked.

He continued examining the leather case and the tools.

"They aren't dental tools. It's a lock-pick set."

"What?"

"Burglars use 'em to break into houses."

"I know what you use a lock-pick set for. I'm not an idiot."

"Well . . ." He grinned, begging me to take him on. I dropped it.

He handed the case to me. It was really quite beat up and obviously well used. There was a huge gash across the tools, marring each one—as if something had scraped across all of them while they were in the case. And one of the tools was missing. I turned the case over in my hand, glaring at it, demanding the sticks of metal to tell me more.

"Audrey, if this stuff really belongs to the burglars, then we'd best get our hides out of here while we still can, and leave the stuff. They'll know someone found this place if we take it."

"Yeah, you're probably right. But these might be clues."

He stood staring at the case in my hands. I looked up at Max.

"But what if they're not? Maybe we should take them to your mom." I hesitated, rolling the case over. "She'd know what to do."

"Maybe we should just leave the stuff here and get the cops."

"We can't get the cops. What if these aren't anything important? I don't want to waste their time."

"Audrey, these could be clues. Someone needs to see this stuff."

I stared at the knife. "You're right. But the burglars could come back before we find someone who will listen to us. Your mom would listen."

I handed Max the knife, and he carefully tucked it into his pocket with the lock-pick set—a silent agreement. I rinsed off my foot in the clear water of the bay and pulled on my shoes. I hobbled through the trees and across the beach as quickly as possible, glancing behind me, half expecting someone to jump out of the shadows.

We crossed the street, carefully avoiding the speeding traffic, and walked in the front door of the dive shop. The buzzer announcing our entry made me jump.

My dad was helping a customer with handheld dive computers. Giving us a quick grin, he returned to the customer, oblivious to my limping, at least for the moment.

I grabbed the cordless from the counter in the back of the store and handed it to Max. He dialed his mom's cell number, waited awhile, and then hung up, clenching his jaw.

"She's got her phone turned off. Maybe she's at home. You up to biking over there?"

"Yeah. Let me grab a couple of Band-Aids or something from the first-aid kit." He nodded, and I grabbed the blue plastic kit from behind the checkout counter and scrounged for a big enough bandage, some extra gauze, and some first-aid cream. Plopping down on the cracked brown chair, I carefully pulled my now somewhat bloody shoe off and bandaged my foot.

"That should do it," I said as I gingerly pressed my foot down on the floor and found it didn't hurt as much. Max trotted outside, and I hobbled behind him. We pulled our bikes out from under the sign and made our way out the back entrance of the parking lot. Max lived only a few blocks east of the store, but he graciously kept the pace slow as I practically one-foot-pedaled the whole way.

Max lived in one of those neighborhoods where all the houses look the same—little squares with two windows and a door in the front, an unattached garage in the back yard, and a little door on the side of the house. The one difference between Max's place and everyone else's was the yard. Max's mom was a great gardener. Her favorite plants—roses—were tastefully placed everywhere. Big yellow roses traced the lines of the fence, and the back of the house was lined with big bushes with tiny red flowers. Though I wouldn't admit it to a soul, as it was too "girly," I loved her roses. They were beautiful and varied but tough—my favorite plant carried cheerful red and white zebra-striped blooms that smelled wonderful, but the stems bore their very own patch of carve-your-fingers-up thorns. Certainly kept *me* away from them.

Max banked into his driveway and dropped his bike, narrowly missing a group of bushes.

"I'll see if she's home real quick," he yelled over his shoulder as the screen door slammed shut. I shook my head at his back and picked up his bike, holding it for him until he came back.

I heard Max's pounding trot move down the stairs toward his bedroom. A few moments later, I heard him screaming at his obnoxious older brother—something about the house being Max's, too—and then I heard footsteps hammering back up the stairs.

Max tripped over the last step and crashed through the doorway. In one movement Max grabbed his bike, leapt onto it, and pedaled out of his driveway.

I didn't have to be told what to do. I moved, fast, completely forgetting my injured foot.

We rounded the corner out of the driveway as Shawn burst through the door yelling at Max. There was another guy's voice mixed into the yelling, but I didn't want to slow down to see who it was. We didn't stop until we reached the park, five blocks down and three over.

Panting, we shoved the front tires of our bikes into the bike rack and stood to catch our breath. I leaned up against the metal frame of the rack and looked at Max. Somewhere along the line, he'd grabbed his soccer ball.

"My mom wasn't home, so I couldn't tell her what was going on."

"What's with the soccer ball?"

"Well, Shawn wanted to know what was going on, so I told him I was grabbing the soccer ball and we were going to the park to play. He didn't believe me."

"That's what all the yelling was about? Your brother can be a real jerk." Up until a few months ago Shawn had been pretty decent. He's a year younger than my brother, but when he got a job with some mysterious friend of his dad's, he got all "grown up" and grouchy when either Max or I breathed wrong. I'm not often thankful for having to live with my too-perfect little sister, but at least she hasn't gone completely psycho on me for no apparent reason.

"Well, we might as well play while we're waiting for your mom to get home. Just take it easy on the injured one." He tossed the ball to me as we scanned the park for an empty place to play. Max pointed to a spot on the far side of the field—half in the shade, half in the sun. I smiled. It was perfect. Max could play in the sun, as he preferred, and I, the fair-skinned wonder that I am, could play in the shade and avoid finding out just how sunburnt a person could get in one afternoon.

We trotted over to our selected area. Playing soccer was one of the many things we both loved to do. When we played as a team against other kids, we ruled the turf. I was excellent on defense—there were few people who could get past me, because I wasn't afraid to throw my body in their path. And Max was a phenomenal attacker—he had perfect timing and placement to make the goalkeepers miss his bullets. But there really wasn't anyone in the park to challenge to a game, so we were content kicking the ball back and forth.

We'd been at it for a few minutes when Max launched a beauty over my head and into the woods behind me. I sighed, silently blamed my injury and allergy-induced sneezes for the miss, and trudged over to the line of trees. Carefully moving the pricker bushes out of my way, I picked my way around the wildflowers, trees, and unidentified slimy green things—no point in adding to the grass stains already on my shorts.

Fortunately for my bare legs, the ball wasn't too far back and was resting just in front of the heaviest undergrowth. I leaned over, grabbed the ball, and started back to the field.

"Cut it out, you jerk." It was Max, and it sounded like he was in trouble. I ran back through the trees and brush, oblivious to the fresh scratches on my legs.

"What's wrong, chink? Little baby want to run home to his mommy?"

"You scared, little slant-eyed sissy?"

I broke through the forest just as a burly kid punched Max in the stomach. Running at full speed, I tackled the nearest kid. He landed with a satisfying "Oof!"

What I hadn't stopped to consider was that there were five of them and two of us.

I rolled over and jumped back up, only to be kicked in the back of the legs and shoved forward. I skidded across the grass on my hands and knees. I'd forgotten how much grass burns hurt. But I didn't have much time to contemplate the thought—another kid was coming for me, his blond hair swishing around his head. As he planted one foot and lifted the other to kick me, I leaned back to avoid the incoming one, using my momentum to twist along the ground and kick at the stationary foot. He landed in a heap in front of me. It gave me a second to find Max. He was already down, with blood coming out of his nose.

There was a pop followed by a *shissss* sound behind me. I twisted around in time to see the biggest guy of the group pulling a rather large knife out of our soccer ball. We were dead meat.

Chapter 5

I didn't often contemplate whether or not God really heard prayers, but I sent up a series of them, trusting God wouldn't ignore two teens about to be demolished.

"Hey, Lucas. Why don't you pick on someone your own size?" Though I never would have said it was possible, I was glad to hear Shawn's voice.

"Great, another chink who's too big for his britches. If you want to play, come over and play," the giant said with a sneer. I gulped. Shawn was a tall guy, but Lucas matched his height and was massive across his shoulders.

Shawn just jerked his head back ever so slightly, pointing to a group of rather rough-looking characters standing behind him. I recognized a few of the guys; I'd seen them with Shawn at one time or another.

I glanced up at the burly guy, finally recognizing the icy blue eyes—Lucas O'Malley. He'd grown over the summer.

Lucas had always bullied me around at school and at church. It wasn't usually anything big, and the moment any adult questioned what was going on, he'd turn on the charm, flip a switch to light his halo, and the inquisitive adult would entirely miss the horns below the circle of cherubic light. But I'd never been truly scared of Lucas—until this moment.

Lucas clenched his jaw and his fist tightened around the knife.

I found myself praying under my breath. *Oh please, Lord, make him walk away. Make him walk away.*

"Just wait until you're alone, chink lover." It took me a moment to realize that his statement and glare were directed at me! I gulped and shivered, aware that he really meant it.

"Move it! Now, Lucas!" It wasn't a command I would ignore, and neither did Lucas.

Maybe it was just the jolt to my hard head, but I had no clue what was happening. How could Shawn stay so calm? Why in the world was Lucas going to kill me? And *Shawn*, our recent archenemy—the intimidating older brother—was saving our lives.

"You guys okay?" He actually sounded and looked concerned.

I heard a moan coming from Max's direction. From my twisted position on the ground, I stumbled to my feet and into a walk-limp. Max looked like he'd run through a medieval torture machine, complete with battering ram. I dropped to the ground.

"Don't move him," Shawn said quickly, as if he were an expert. "If he's broken something, it will only make things worse."

"I didn't break anything, Shawn. One of them just hit me square in the nose. I'm still seeing little blue spots."

Max lifted his head and rolled into a sitting position. He had blood splatters on his white T-shirt and jean shorts. His normally sleek black hair was matted with dirt and grass. There was a trickle of blood running down his heart-shaped face, threatening to merge with the stream at his nose and cause a flood. And one of his eyes, which he was rubbing, was just a slit, barely open. Max blinked and rolled his eyes, obviously trying to focus.

When he turned to look at me, he inhaled sharply. Apparently I looked as bad as he did, which immediately shifted my concern from Lucas to my mom. Mom never liked me acting "unladylike," let alone approving of an all-out fight. She was going to kill me, or at least bring me within an inch of my life, before Lucas and crew could try again.

"You look awful, Audrey."

"You should talk, my friend."

"Yeah, I know." Max looked up at Shawn. "So, where'd you come from?" It was a good question. Ignoring the pain in my neck, I looked back at Shawn, curious to know the answer to Max's question.

"Nowhere. We were just on our way to the baseball game when we saw Lucas prowling around. Since you took the soccer ball, I figured you guys were out here, and I know how much Lucas *loves* our family. So, you know."

As if *that* made sense. For one thing, Shawn hated baseball on principle—their dad, whom they despised for several good reasons, loved the game. For another, the only game being played was a Little League game. What interest would a college freshman have in that? But I wasn't about to press the issue. I'd already run headfirst into trouble today; I didn't need to start anything with the guy who'd just rescued us. Despite what my mom apparently thinks, I do learn my lesson sometimes.

Besides, Shawn hadn't given me much time to ponder his bizarre response. After a quick shrug of his narrow shoulders, he trotted back to his group of friends with a dismissive "I'll see you at home for dinner."

I watched them until they disappeared beyond the baseball diamond. I looked at Max.

"That was weird. What's up with him? And why does Lucas have a thing against your family?"

Max was just staring straight ahead. He took a deep breath and pushed himself off the ground.

"It's just a family thing."

A family thing between Lucas and Shawn. Was I that dim-witted? It seemed that sidestepping pointed questions was also a family thing. My life had just been threatened at knife point by a jerk spouting decidedly politically incorrect Asian slurs (which, by the way, only proved his complete lack of intelligence—Max and his family were not Chinese or Japanese), and all of this was just because of some "family thing." Yeah, right.

But the word *whatever* is actually what came out from between my broken lips. It was the best I could do under the circumstances. I stood up and retrieved the destroyed ball. Turning it over in my hand, I shook my head. Summer break was not looking good.

"Let's go to my house and wait for my mom to get home. I hurt too much to move, let alone kick a flat soccer ball."

I turned and hobbled toward my bike. My head hurt too much to think of anything better to do. Realizing he wasn't following me, I turned back to face him. "What?" I asked.

"We need to clean up before we go home. I don't want to freak anyone out."

I raised my eyebrow in contempt until he stalked over and shoved my face in front of a car's mirror.

My dark hair was sticking up at odd angles, and in combination with the grass and dirt that sprang from the peaks and valleys, it gave me a strangely angular look, like some weird piece of abstract art. The blood that I had tasted earlier was beginning to crust in the corner of my mouth, which was now puffy from one of my not-so-elegant landings. But the worst thing was the rather large bump starting to swell on the right side of my forehead.

I frowned at myself in the mirror. He had a good point. Good enough for me to concede this small defeat. He grinned at me as we headed toward the baseball diamond and the bathrooms.

Once a little cleaner, we snatched up our bikes and began slowly pedaling out of the park. My body protested the movement, but walking would take twice the time and be nearly as painful. At the road, we dutifully looked both ways; my lazy glance to the left started my body shaking. It was Lucas and his goons again. They were all standing around talking.

With my legs still straddling my beat-up blue bike, I carefully duck-waddled backward to the weeping willow, just back from the road. In my condition, I wasn't ashamed to hide. Max, confused, followed my look. Out of the corner of my eye I could see Max cautiously moving back toward me in the same duck-waddle I'd used. Then he stopped, one foot on the pedal, ready to make a fast escape if necessary.

"Look at that bike," I whispered, shaking my head half in jealousy, half in anger. "It's a brand new mountain bike. That must have cost him a fortune."

"His dad probably bought it for him."

But we both knew that wasn't true. It was true that Mr. O'Malley, who owned several ritzy art galleries and even the art museum at Northwestern, was beyond rich. But he also was a legendary tightwad. Where in the world had Lucas gotten the money for that bike?

Lucas and his band of thugs, their discussion finished, jumped on their bikes and headed away from us. Max let out his breath and pedaled out into the street. I followed, retracing our earlier path to the little square house.

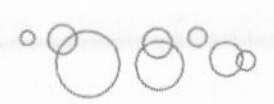

At Max's house, we were in for another surprise. Shawn's beat-up white station wagon with fake wood paneling sat to the right of the one-car garage. So much for the Little League game—he'd already come home. Weird, if you ask me. But no one had given me permission to stick my nose in, so, for once, I kept my mouth neatly shut.

We kicked off our shoes and socks before going into the house. I dutifully waited on the welcome mat while Max retrieved a pair of non-bloody socks for me. The spotless cream-colored carpet demanded clean feet at all times. Shawn wasn't in the kitchen. He must have been downstairs.

I found myself tiptoeing and whispering. I didn't feel like having another run-in.

"What's for dinner?"

"Tacos, I think. You hungry?"

"Yeah."

Max opened the fridge, pulled out the hamburger his mom had been thawing, and dropped it into the pan on the stove. The tacos were well on their way when I heard movement in the basement. I guessed it was Shawn.

"I already told you I'd be there and that I'd take care of Lucas O'Malley for you. He won't stick his nose in our business for a while." Before my mind could fully form the thought *Who's he talking to?* it occurred to me that we were listening to a conversation that Shawn would likely want to be private. I heard footsteps on the stairs.

There was no way this could turn out well.

"I'll make the delivery tonight. . . . Look, you don't need to worry about me." Shawn turned around the corner and stepped into the kitchen. "What the—! I gotta go."

I hated being right.

He lunged around me to grab Max by the shirt and shove him against the wall. Max lost his balance, tripping over the step behind him and landing hard on the floor of the living room.

"What are you little twerps doing here?" Shawn stood over Max, displaying all the height he'd gotten from his father.

Max struggled to get up. I stared intently at the tiny rose pattern on the kitchen linoleum.

"It's my house, too, Shawn."

"That doesn't give you the right to listen in on a private conversation, does it?" Shawn stepped back and I scrambled to stay out of his way. Playground bullies I at least *thought* I could deal with, but Shawn was another story. And it wasn't just that he was unusually tall and muscular both for his eighteen years and his Asian genes—he also had a way of getting to me and making me back down. I wanted to stand up for Max, but I had suddenly lost my ever-present voice.

Chapter 6

Shawn grabbed Max again and was about to throw him against the counter in front of me, when the screen door creaked.

"Boys!" That one word thundered through the hallway. It should have been the shout of our massive-sized school principal, a cop, or at least a person who *looked* threatening. But, no, it was the voice of just-under-five-foot Mrs. Myer. Though she looked like she wouldn't be able to get the better of a housefly, she was one tough gal who demanded, and received, respect. And it wasn't just her reputation as a no-nonsense crime reporter that made people pay attention.

The standoff that followed reminded me of the moment in a professional wrestling match just after the referee announces the contestants.

In this corner, weighing in at 175 pounds and 110 pounds, the Myer boys. In this corner, weighing in at 90 pounds, Mom.

Shawn stood snarling at his mom over Max's head. Max just stood stone still, his face pale.

The boys didn't have a chance.

"Shawn, to your room. Max, Audrey, to the table."

She brushed past all of us as we stood there dumbly. As if nothing had happened, she dropped her soft leather briefcase and black, functional purse on the floor next to the table. Shawn was the first to move. With one final swat to the back of Max's head, he stomped back to the entryway and down the stairs to his room. My "guaranteed to shrivel anyone" glare just bounced off the back of Shawn's head. I'd get him later . . . maybe.

Mrs. Myer sighed and turned back toward us. She was in lecture mode. But the moment she caught sight of me, her previous concern was gone.

"Aud! What in the world happened? Did Shawn . . . ?"

I'd almost forgotten about the mangled face thing.

"Oh! No, it wasn't him. Lucas O'Malley and his thugs were in the park and took offense at Max and me being alive and decided to press their point. No big deal. We're both okay."

She looked at me hard with that quizzical look parents get when they're trying to figure out whether or not you're telling them everything.

"Lucas O'Malley." I could see Mrs. Myer thumbing through her memories. "Isn't he . . . ?" She left the question hanging when Max grunted and looked at her with a "Be quiet, Mom" look.

"You'd better let me take you home." I knew that move. She was changing the subject to avoid the questions she'd raised in her own mind. I was curious about how she knew Lucas, but I was more than happy to let the subject of my beating drop. On the other hand, the last thing I wanted to do was to go home. But just saying I didn't want to go wouldn't prevent the parent code of sending a kid home when she got a bump or bruise from being enforced.

"That's okay. My dad said it was okay to come over here." It was the truth, and she didn't have to know that he hadn't seen my puffy lip and lumpy forehead.

"Well, at least let me get you some ice." Apparently the incident with Shawn had been forgotten. Maybe it had to do with one of the stories she'd researched for her former job as the health reporter at the *Port Haven Record Eagle,* but Mrs. Myer was second only to my mom for knowing the best thing to do for every injury. So I let her crush up some ice, place it in a baggy, and press it against my damaged body, effectively freezing my lips and skull. If nothing else, I reasoned, maybe they'd go numb and wouldn't throb quite as badly.

She neatly installed Max and me at the kitchen table with matching baggies of ice. It wasn't until a few minutes later that the smell of ground beef burning reminded us all about dinner. Jumping up, she cranked the gas off and yanked the yellow pan off the matching yellow stove in one swift motion that would have made any professional baseball player proud.

Setting the pan on the cool side of the stove, she turned, pulled the shells out of the pantry next to the refrigerator, poured some juice, and set the table for four. Enough for all of us, including Shawn.

Max's mom leaned around the corner and threw her voice down the stairs. "Shawn! Time for dinner."

"Not hungry," came the muffled reply.

Mrs. Myer's gaze dropped to the floor, and she shrugged her shoulders. I shook my head at the thought of Shawn. He could be such a dim-witted jerk. Yes, he'd rescued us this afternoon, but he still didn't have a clue about how much his mom tried. Mrs. Myer sat at the head of the table to my left, bowed her head, and mumbled something to the effect of, "Lord, bless this food and our house. Amen."

It always surprised me that she prayed. Every once in a while, Max came to church with my family, but the Myers never went to church together. Max said that they had attended before his dad left the family five years ago. Maybe it had something to do with that. But no one ever had told me why Mr. Myer left or why they didn't go to church anymore, and I hadn't gotten up enough nerve to ask.

The only sound in the kitchen was that of us munching on the slightly charred meat, which had been crammed into shattering taco shells and covered with cheese. It was depressing. Usually you couldn't shut this family up. I had to do something.

"So, do you know Lucas?" From the sharp kick Max gave me, I had obviously stumbled on the wrong "something."

"Mark used to run one of the art galleries for Lucas's father." *Max's dad was an art dealer?* It explained the immaculately decorated apartment Max was forced to visit every other weekend. I'd always had trouble putting the somewhat scruffy, flannel-shirt-wearing, scrawny man together with the apartment he kept. The apartment was always spotless and was the exact opposite of his personal appearance.

Max said his dad worked from home doing international imports for the same guy Shawn now worked for. I had no idea what "international imports" meant, and I wanted to ask. I even opened my mouth to do that. But the sight of Mrs. Myer pushing around her food with a broken taco shell kept my mouth shut on the subject.

The window air conditioner in the other room kicked on and made me jump. I still hadn't fixed the too-quiet problem.

"So, how was work?" It was a lame question, but it might work. Since she'd taken over some of the hard-news reporting, Mrs. Myer had worked on a lot of exciting stories. She looked at me and sighed.

"Actually, pretty interesting." She obviously wanted a subject change, so she took the opportunity. "I've been interviewing the police about a string of house burglaries up and down the lakeshore. The thieves weren't doing much at first—stealing a stereo or television here and there. But they've recently been linked to a few armed robberies that have turned pretty violent. Fortunately, no one's been killed, but they're getting gutsy, and that only means trouble."

Like I said, it was fascinating stuff, and her reluctance to talk started to fade. As she told us about the gang, her deep brown eyes started to flash a bit, her short, wavy hair swayed back and forth with her head, and her small hands moved constantly, almost as though she were using them to direct her thoughts out into the open.

Even in her most "parental" moments, Mrs. Meyer was generally pretty cool. Some days I wished my mom could be more like Max's mom. Interesting and comfortable. Sophisticated, but practical.

Max said his mom had actually been born in Cambodia, and that she and her parents were part of a small group of people who had escaped the country. From what I could gather, Mrs. Myer and her family were sponsored by some local Christians, and they arrived here when Mrs. Myer was six or seven—about Suzie's age. Maybe everything she went through as a little kid somehow made her cooler than the average parent. Regardless of why, she was almost as fun as anyone my age.

I smiled as she told about the police beginning to narrow down the number of suspects who may have been leading the group. She'd been able to track down one of the staging areas for the gang—a group of abandoned cottages on the south side of town. But since the last incident, the police weren't talking, or didn't know anything more, and she hadn't found any new clues at the station or the old crime scenes. So she was planning on trying to pull in a few favors on Monday in an effort to track down the guys the cops had on their list. It wasn't until she told us she'd been concentrating on figuring out the symbol they left at every scene that Max remembered our clues.

"Oh! I almost forgot." Max grabbed his napkin and used it to pull out the knife we'd found. "It has the same symbol on it as the one they've been leaving behind."

Her eyes widened in a mix of concern and excitement when she saw the knife. "Where did you guys find this?"

"It was in the woods by the lake," Max said. "We found it next to one of those big black drums Dad used to anchor buoys to."

Mrs. Myer blinked. It was a much too-controlled reaction. I was trying to figure out how to ask her what she was thinking when the side door slammed shut, jolting me out of my chair. Shawn had just stormed out of the house. I hadn't even heard him come up the stairs.

Looking across the table at Max, I cocked an eyebrow. Max barely shook his head. We weren't going to talk about it now. We both turned toward his mom so that she could finish her story, but the spell had been broken.

"Max, please clean up the table," Mrs. Myer whispered as she pushed away from the table.

Max scrambled out of his chair, grabbed the plates and silverware off the table, and began rinsing them off before dropping them into the dishwasher.

Mrs. Myer paused before standing up. "Do you want a ride home, Audrey?" Her voice came from far away—the place her thoughts were, I suppose.

"Yeah, that'd be great," I said a heartbeat too quickly, now desperate to escape the tension and talk to Max adult-free.

"Let me just change, and I'll be right back." In a brief real-world moment, she shot us what I can only describe as the mom look for "You'd better not be up to anything." She nodded, walked down the hallway just outside of the dining room, and softly closed the door to her bedroom.

I gulped and turned to Max.

"What're you up to, Audrey?" Max had an almost parental look on his face, too.

"What's the big deal? I just wanted to talk to you about what we're going to do tomorrow."

His silence told me he didn't believe me.

"Okay, so I want to explore a little bit tomorrow."

"Audrey, you and I both know our parents would kill us if they found out we might be interfering with a police investigation. These guys are really dangerous. Besides, what could we do?"

The phone rang, cutting off my retort. He grabbed the phone before I could try to convince him to keep looking into things, but not before he threw me another look that could have made the lake boil.

"Hello?" He clenched his jaw and turned his back on me, as if trying to prevent me from seeing the caller.

"Oh. Hi, Dad," he mumbled. "No, he's not home. He just left. He's probably on his way over to your place now."

"Hello?" Max took the phone away from his ear and squinted at it as if he could see his dad on the other side. "Well, I guess that's good-bye." He'd been hung up on. The phone beeped as he clicked it off.

Well, the call had prevented an argument for the moment, but now it was just awkward silence.

From what Max had said, Shawn was hanging out more and more with his dad. We both had agreed, without really talking about it, that Shawn's new fascination with Mr. Myer was very strange. After all, Shawn wouldn't even speak to his dad until a few months ago. The only thing we could figure was that the guy Shawn was working for was a friend and business associate of Mr. Myer's. He had to be nice to keep his cushy job.

"You okay?"

"Yeah."

His mom's door opened before I could form a response.

"Let's go, guys."

Mrs. Myer grabbed her purse from the floor by the fridge and held the door open for Max and me to walk through.

By the time we got home I had almost entirely forgotten that my face had been slightly rearranged.

When my mom saw me, her eyes grew huge and her mouth worked but no words came out. Suzie, who was perched perfectly on the piano bench, no doubt practicing without being asked, exactly duplicated my mother's look of horror.

It was a good thing Mrs. Myer had brought me home. . . . Mom had to be polite in front of other people.

She tightly thanked Mrs. Myer for dropping me off and spun to close the door half a second before it was polite to do so. I started to explain, but Mom was too busy rambling at the top of her lungs about me being someone else's daughter, sitting me none too gently down at the table, and getting me ice, to really listen to my story.

Suzie trailed behind her and handed her a towel to wrap the ice in at the exact moment my mom reached for it.

I could see my mom mentally comparing me to Suzie. Me in my ripped jean shorts, tattered face, and out-of-control hair. Suzie in her pink lacy pajamas, rosy cheeks, and ringlets piled perfectly on top of her head. *Go away, brat.*

Dad finally made his way down the stairs to explore the commotion. He wasn't thrilled with my new look either, but at least he listened to me and began trying to sooth Mom.

I could hear Dad quietly explaining that it wasn't my fault and that I was just standing up for my friend. From the kitchen, Mom gave me a sideways squinty look that said she only half believed me, and then handed me the bag of crushed ice.

"Thanks," I muttered, trying hard to sound grateful. What good would it do to use ice hours after the incident *and* after I'd already been iced down once? I didn't even have a headache anymore. But I put the bag to my forehead anyway. Mom used to work as a nurse at the local hospital, and I didn't want to risk her thinking I didn't trust her judgment.

Dad sat down next to me, then pulled me into his lap. I leaned back. Safe at last.

"Audrey," he sighed. "I know you were trying to help your friend, but you need to learn to control your temper." He turned me a little so that I was forced to look into his eyes. "You could've been hurt badly, and I don't want that to happen. We're not going to ground you, but consider yourself on probation. Another stunt like this, and your mom and I will have no choice. Understand?"

I looked down at his arms holding me tightly, and nodded.

"Does probation mean I can't go to Max's tomorrow?"

I could see Mom out of the corner of my eye. She looked mad, but she was deferring to Dad. "You can go over to his house if his mom says it's okay. In fact, how about if you and Max come to the store tomorrow? I could use your help. And maybe I can get away long enough to take you guys down for a quick dive."

I started to smile but stopped it before it reached my lips. I didn't want to upset my mom any more. She was going to let me go over to Max's tomorrow; I wasn't grounded. I didn't want to push my luck.

Chapter 7

I woke up to bright sunshine and my dad shuffling out the door, grumbling about having to man the store again.

Jumping out of bed, I took a quick shower, pulled on a pair of old jean shorts and a T-shirt, and ran downstairs.

Mom looked up as I walked into the kitchen and simply handed me a bowl and the box of cereal without comment. It was obvious that she'd wanted a grounding and hadn't gotten it. I grabbed the milk out of the fridge and scarfed down the cold cereal.

"Thanks, Mom." I got a flat smile in response. She wasn't impressed. I added, "I'll be at Max's if you need me for anything." Before she could second-guess last night's decision, I was out the back door. I jumped on my bike and made my way to Max's.

I knocked on the door and heard a muffled "Who is it?" come from the basement. Carefully resting my bike on the cement step to the back door, I opened the screen, announced my arrival, and ran down the stairs to the basement.

"I—I'm in the laundry room." Max, the ever-responsible one, was doing chores . . . on a Saturday. I was so perturbed with the perfect-son routine that I nearly missed the fear in Max's voice.

I stomped across the family room, yanked open the laundry-room door, and found Max slumped against the washing machine, tears rolling down his face and his fingers wrapped tightly around what looked like a metal object.

"Max?"

His fingers unclenched one at a time. Resting in the palm of his hand was a knife, just like the one we'd found at the beach.

"It was in Shawn's pocket." He said it like it was a death sentence.

"Maybe he just found the one we gave your mom."

"Mom put it in her locked briefcase to take to the police. She's gonna bring it to Chief Minard."

I crumpled to the floor beside him.

"Max, this doesn't necessarily mean—"

"Audrey, my brother's one of them."

"It could be anything. Maybe your mom forgot it. Or . . . or maybe she found another one at a crime scene and that's the one she took to the chief."

"My mom wouldn't willfully keep evidence from the police."

Okay, I knew that, but there had to be an explanation. Whatever it was, I didn't want to wait for Shawn to come in and find us in his business again.

"Max, it couldn't be your brother. If he were stealing a ton of stuff, he'd have enough money to buy something better than that dumpy station wagon he drives." I was scrambling for something, anything.

"I mean, it'd more likely be Lucas. Remember that bike he had? It must have cost him more than your brother's car is worth. And we both know his dad wouldn't buy it for him. Besides, your brother's a decent guy when you get down to it. He doesn't go around picking on everyone. He wouldn't do this."

Max sat clutching his knees to his chest. I wasn't getting anywhere, and I was beginning to get a familiar shaky feeling in my stomach.

"Max, take a deep breath. If Shawn finds us in here with the knife and it *is* his, we're dead."

The chirping of a phone in Shawn's room next door made me freeze. He was in there and now he was probably awake.

The sound was muffled, but I could make out a few words here and there. Shawn was talking to his dad.

Then suddenly he switched to what must have been Khmer.

Interested, I glanced at Max and whispered, "I didn't know your dad could speak Khmer."

"Neither did I." I gulped and scrambled to my feet, pulling Max with me. Before tiptoeing up the stairs, I pulled the knife from Max's hand and dropped it into Shawn's laundry basket.

Safely upstairs, Max fell into a kitchen chair, looking defeated.

"What were they talking about?"

"Shawn was promising that he'd finish the job tonight."

"Good morning, Audrey!" Boy was I ever on edge lately. Mrs. Myer's cheery greeting had about sent me through the plastered ceiling.

"How are you guys doing this morning?"

Finding my composure and shooting Max a warning look, I calmly answered that we were fine and asked what she planned to do that day. I was tempted to tell Mrs. Myer about Shawn, but we had to be sure he was involved first. It'd kill her to think that her son might be involved in the worst burglaries the county had seen in a long time.

"Well, not only did the police conclude that the group uses those old abandoned cottages just down from your dad's dive shop, there were some airtight barrels in the buildings, just like the one you guys found. I'm guessing they're putting the electronics they're stealing in the barrels for transportation and storage.

"I already had one of the guys check out the place you kids found, and there wasn't anything there anymore. My guess is that they've scattered the barrels, hiding them until they need them for the next job. I'm going to see if I can figure out where they're dropping the barrels. Maybe there are still some around. I know the police need a lead, and quickly—before these guys really hurt someone."

Max shoved away from the table, threw his bowl into the sink, and stormed out the side door. As the bowl clattered around, finally settling on the stainless steel, Mrs. Myer raised her eyebrows at me. I erased the guilt from my face and shrugged my shoulders.

"Well, you two have fun and be careful. I'll have my cell on if you need me." She didn't have to add, "And stay away from where you found that knife"—her clenched jaw and dark eyes said everything.

I blinked my understanding and followed Max out the door.

"Audrey, we have to tell my mom."

"We don't know your brother is involved, Max. We can't accuse him of this without knowing for sure." He grimaced, shaking his head firmly.

"Max, it'd kill your mom." That did it. His head dropped in silent agreement.

"Come on, let's go down to the ice cream shop. I'll buy." I pushed his bike toward him. He nodded, just barely, and swung his leg over the bike.

Joe's Ice Cream Shop was just behind the dive shop and had the best ice cream around. We both ordered our favorites, in freshly made waffle cones, and sat down on the shop's steps.

The sun floated in and out of the clouds, casting shadows across Max's face, as we sat quietly slurping our ice cream.

"What am I going to do, Audrey? What if Shawn's in on this?" Okay, the ice cream was supposed to have helped stop his worrying. Wasn't it the cure-all food?

"Well, we could investigate ourselves, Max, but you don't want to do that."

"That's not fair, Audrey."

Okay, so I was manipulating him a bit, but I wanted to know what was going on as much as he did.

"You're right. Sorry. What do you want to do then?"

"I suppose it wouldn't hurt to look down by the beach again."

"Your mom said that they'd checked down there last night and didn't find anything. Besides, she all but told us to stay away from there." I'm told this technique is called reverse psychology. Whatever the lingo, it works. His clenched jaw told me he had made up his mind.

"Let's go then," I added, as if conceding defeat. Pushing our bikes alongside us, we walked across the grass adjacent to the Corner Mall and started down toward the beach.

It took us a grand total of five minutes to walk over to the woods to see nothing but a dent in the ground, collecting water—an imprint of where the barrel had been.

"Nothing."

Max looked at me, his fists clenched by his side. I didn't know what we'd expected to see—maybe a blinking sign saying, "Shawn's in on it!" I guess that was a little too much to ask for.

"Got any ideas?" he asked, defeat in his voice. I trotted up behind him.

"He isn't in on it, Max." I could have been talking to a brick wall. "We could check out the cottages where your mom said the cops had found more barrels." I was surprised to realize it, but I believed what I'd said about Shawn. Don't ask me why. It was just something I had to believe. Despite how mean Shawn had become in the last few months, he was still Mrs. Myer's son. He was still a guy who cared enough to stick up for his little brother. And he was the guy who used to let me ride around town on the handlebars of his bike. A pain? Yes. A hardened criminal? Something inside me said no.

I expected him to object, but he made a tight turn and walked back toward the cottages across the street. His shoulders slumped forward as he slipped and stumbled up the slope. I tried not to notice him swiping at his eyes. Guys never like to have anyone see them cry. I felt a bit like a nosy aunt, but I swung my arm around him and smiled into his grimace.

"We'll figure it out, Max. No matter what Shawn is like to us, this isn't him."

Max just shrugged off my arm and dodged the cars as he crossed the street.

Chapter 8

I watched my feet move to follow him. Heel, toe, push off. Avoid the sidewalk bump pushed up by the roots of the old maple. Heel, toe, push off. Cross the street. Heel, toe, push off.

We turned the bend; I was right behind Max . . . a little lost puppy trailing after my best friend and his fears. A car zoomed by, forcing Max to stop—and I, still watching my feet, stepped onto the back of his heel. He jumped and I mumbled something along the lines of, "Sorry."

"Now what?" His voice had an edge that I'd never heard before. I stood staring at the line of cottages. The windows stood empty, glaring back at me and muttering their agreement with Max.

I stepped across the street and onto what I'd guess someone once considered a lawn. The wind groaned through the maple tree around the corner. The first house was missing the steps once leading to the front door, so I grasped the wobbly railing surrounding the porch and put half my weight on the concrete slab. When the crumbling around the railing didn't bring the whole house down around me, I heaved myself up to stand in front of the door.

I don't know what I expected when I reached out to open the door, but I don't think it had registered that everything would be boarded up kid-proof tight. And it wasn't just the front door that was reinforced with crisscrossed lumber and layers of spider webbing. It also was the windows, garage door, and back door. The lattice that led up to the second-story was broken up so much that even I didn't attempt to climb it.

"Audrey?" I turned around to find that Max wasn't behind me any longer. I stepped out of the shadow of the first house.

"Max?" I yelled down the street.

"Audrey?" This time it came louder and was tinged with concern. Trotting down the street, I glanced around each house.

I found Max at the back of the fifth and last abandoned cottage on the cul-de-sac. He was standing on the cracked concrete of the driveway, staring just beyond a familiar-looking black barrel at his feet. I trotted up next to him and stopped abruptly when my gaze locked on the object of Max's unwavering attention; we both were staring into the golden eyes of a rather large, black dog. Now I love dogs as much as the next person, but at the moment, I wasn't feeling all that close to Jaws, the dog, who was apparently measuring my leg for lunch.

"Don't run." It was my own brand of oh-so-stupid wisdom.

"Yeah. Already not doing that."

I took a step back and the growling dropped a bit in pitch.

"Try talking to it, Audrey. Dogs like you."

"Nice dog." I had barely squeaked it out when the dog lunged and I promptly forgot my "no running" recommendation and ran for my life.

I'd only gotten five steps when the dog latched onto my shoulder. Screaming, I swung around and clocked Max in the chest.

Coughing in surprise, Max doubled over, clutching his shirt and pointing back at the dog, which was lunging on the end of its chain. Oh. It hadn't been the dog at all.

Being that the barrel was out of the reach of Jaws, Max tiptoed back to the barrel and dragged it around the corner so we could investigate without further angering our new friend.

It wasn't until Max started playing with the lining of the barrel that I became aware of the absence of police tape. Odd. If the cops considered this a crime scene, where was the shiny yellow tape declaring, "Police Line. Do Not Cross"?

I pointed this out to Max, who just grunted and continued poking at the barrel.

"There's silica in the lining." He declared it as if the little cream-colored beads he was rolling around in his hands solved everything.

"Isn't that the stuff they put in the boxes of new shoes to keep moisture out or something?"

Max just nodded and stared at his hands. "Why would they put silica in the lining?" I had no idea, but the sound of the dog trying to rip free of its bondage convinced me we needed to move quickly.

"Let's take the barrel to your mom. Maybe she'll know."

"No, you're right. The police didn't put tape out on purpose. They probably didn't want to tip off the burglars." He stuffed a few of the little beads into his pocket and without looking at me, started walking away. "I need to go home and finish the laundry and stuff before my mom gets home. But she said we could still do something later." Something was up. I didn't know what. I had no problem leaving behind the dog, but I wasn't sure about the barrel.

A loud snap from the back of the house made me reconsider, and we speed-walked our way back to the main street. I turned around once to see a tall man in a flannel shirt walking—or, more accurately, being half-dragged by—Jaws down the street in the opposite direction. The dog's owner apparently had been there the whole time, but he didn't seem to care what we were up to. I swallowed hard, tried to act normal, and let Max follow me back to the dive shop.

Max dug his bike out from our hiding place by the sign while I sat on the concrete sidewalk, unwilling to completely forget about the barrel.

I gazed back down the street we had just left to see a red convertible scream away.

I couldn't believe it—it was Mr. Broome. What in the world was he doing here?

I looked up to see Max staring down the street, too. "Isn't he supposed to be halfway around the world, diving?" As usual, Max was saying what I was thinking.

"I don't know. Maybe my dad can answer that." I pulled open the side door to the shop, letting Max walk inside. As I turned to enter myself, Lucas sped by on his brand-new, ultra-expensive bike. I slipped quickly through the entry to avoid being seen and nearly ran Max over. He was standing just inside the door, waiting for me to turn on the lights.

Lights. The equipment room was dark. Dad never left all the lights off. It was too easy to trip over something. I flipped on the light and frowned into the now bright room. Nothing seemed out of place.

"Dad?" I called into the room and hugged my elbows. "Dad?"

I turned toward a muffled voice coming from my dad's office. We walked around the shelving unit and hanging rods to my dad's office door. I knocked and slowly creaked the door open.

The overhead light was off but Dad's desktop light was on, creating an odd silhouette of dad. His phone was tucked carefully under his ear. As he discussed a dive vacation with one of the local divers, he swiveled toward the open door and smiled grimly at me. Boy was I ever creeping myself out over nothing. It looked like Dad just had a migraine, and I'm thinking that the burglars had hit the dive shop.

But it was still weird that Mr. Broome was in Port Haven and not halfway around the world. I closed the door quietly.

"Let's look in his locker. Maybe something's there that will explain what's going on."

"Whose locker?"

"Mr. Broome's."

"Audrey, I think that's illegal. And what's going to be in his locker that will tell us why he didn't go to Cambodia? You don't think *he's* one of them, do you?"

"I'm not breaking in. I've got the master key." I walked across the equipment room to the second-to-last cubicle and dug through the rental gloves stashed there. "See?" I displayed the key for him. "And why couldn't he be one of them?" I raised my eyebrows in a challenge.

"Why would Mr. Broome, a lawyer with a huge bank account, steal electronics from his neighbors around the lake?" He paused, drilling me with his eyes. "I'm going out front."

"Aren't you curious?"

"About what? If that was Mr. Broome and his car, there's likely a good explanation. He's your dad's best dive instructor. Remember?"

"How do you know that his whole trip wasn't a plot to create an alibi?" Sure it was a stretch, but it was yet another option that didn't lead to Shawn.

"Audrey, the cops would be able to figure that out in a heartbeat. They aren't stupid. If he didn't get on the plane as planned, that'd ruin his so-called alibi."

"Maybe." It seemed like a small problem to me. I inserted the small master key into the silver lock in the middle of the combination dial and twisted. I heard the lock open. "See? It's that easy." I swung the door open wide for Max to see my grand discovery of exactly nothing.

"Told you." He sighed and walked around the rows of gear and through the archway to the store, obviously expecting me to follow him.

"Yeah, whatever," I said, closing the locker and digging down through the gloves again. "Ouch. What the . . . " I carefully closed my fingers around the offending item in the glove bin and pulled it out. It was a lock pick. Not just *a* lock pick. *The* missing lock pick. It had the same scratch on it as the ones we'd found earlier.

"There's no way," I whispered to myself. "No way." A war began raging in my mind. If it was the same lock pick we'd found at the beach, that meant that one of the burglars might have been in Dad's shop . . . and it really could have been Mr. Broome.

But then I remembered Lucas speeding by and the guy in the flannel shirt. Mr. Broome would have a legitimate reason to be near the shop, but Lucas and the owner of Jaws? They didn't.

Besides, why would Mr. Broome have blown his cover by showing up where he, and his car, would have been known? But he was supposed to be halfway around the world right now. And if he had been working at the shop, why did he park in the cul-de-sac with the abandoned cottages?

Now I was just confused. I didn't really have anything to tell anyone. And if I told what little I did know, or even suspected, this place would be wrapped in police tape for the next month. I knew there was no way my parents could afford to have the shop down that long during peak diving season.

And what was up with the silica gel stuff? The barrels were already watertight enough to protect electronics during a getaway in a boat. Why take the time to line the barrels with stuff to remove water? Unless they were dropping the barrels into the water. Then water droplets would form on the inside of the barrel like they did in my mask when I dove to a deeper, colder depth.

I wouldn't be able to look anyone in the eyes ever again if I jumped to a conclusion. But if the burglars really were dropping stuff in the lake, then maybe it was near where Max and I had found the barrel. Maybe we'd find something to clarify everything.

"What are you doing?" It was Max.

"Nothing," I claimed, quickly palming the lock pick and trying to look as innocent as possible.

He cocked an eyebrow at me but didn't say anything as he turned back into the shop, giving me a chance to stash the lock pick again. He'd make me give it to my dad, and that'd open a box I wouldn't be able to close.

"I think we should go down directly out from the beach and search for hidden barrels."

Max just looked at me. I could see he was thinking about something else entirely.

"I'm serious." I explained my theory to him.

"Go diving. Alone. On your hunch." It was a *no* I decided to ignore.

"Well, yeah." I said it matter-of-factly, hoping I sounded confident.

"How can I say no clearly enough that you'll listen to me?" He held up his hand in a "just stand there and listen" gesture. "'A,' we're not supposed to dive on our own. 'B,' my mom told me to stay out of the investigation. And 'C,' if there is something down there and it does belong to the burglars, what are you going to do?"

"Bring it up." I couldn't figure out why he was suddenly so against investigating. He didn't play the mom card on me when we were at the cottage. This was the next logical step. We found where they kept the "before-burglary barrel." Now we just had to find where they kept the "just-after-burglary barrel."

His grunt was probably meant as a no, but I took it as a slightly open door.

"I'm serious," I said, scrambling across the back room behind him. "We can take lift bags down with us and bring up whatever's down there."

"Audrey, even if we could get our gear out from under your dad's nose, it's dangerous to dive by ourselves, let alone mess around with a dangerous burglary investigation." Now he was sounding absolutely parental.

"Well, you'll be fifteen in a couple of months. You're practically fully certified. And we won't get caught—no one really dives there. Besides, Ben dove all the time before he turned fifteen and never got caught." My older brother had taught me all of his tricks before he left for college, I explained. His plans even included how to get the gear out of the dive shop, how to go in, get out, and how to return the gear to the dive shop soaking wet and hang it to dry where no one would find it. It was a fail-proof plan that Max couldn't possibly refuse.

"No way." Max shoved the back door of the shop open with a little more force than necessary. "I'm going home, Audrey. I don't feel like hanging out today." He was acting as if diving were something completely out of the ordinary.

It wasn't, really. We were both junior-certified divers. We'd both made a million and one dives. We just weren't supposed to go without an adult.

And we weren't really pursuing the robberies. We were just looking for barrels at the bottom of the lake, barrels that *might* belong to the burglars. I stood inside the door, refusing to give in.

"We've dived a hundred times without incident." I could see he was cracking.

"Whatcha guys up to?"

If it was possible for your heart to vacate your body, mine just had. That's not necessarily a sign of guilt, is it?

"Nothing, Dad," I hedged, trying to think of something intelligent to say. Anything. "We thought we saw Mr. Broome leaving and wondered if you knew what was up." That would do.

Max's look growled at me. Apparently he thought I was crazy.

"No, he's still in Cambodia."

Max smirked and mouthed, "Told ya."

"That's odd. I could have sworn it was him."

"I'm afraid not," Dad said, turning back to his office. Almost as an afterthought, he turned back around. "What are you guys up to today?"

"I don't know; maybe we'll just go swimming later," I lied, dreams of diving the beach dancing in my head.

"I have to go to my dad's this afternoon." Max contradicted me with a not-so-subtle glare.

"I suppose I'm coming with." It was a question that came out as a statement.

Max just shrugged. We were both doomed to an afternoon with his dad.

Chapter 9

It's not that Max's dad is an awful person, I just don't like him very much. He's considerably taller than my dad. He tries really hard to be fun, but his "bachelor pad," which overlooks the shimmering Lake Michigan, has the feel of a museum.

And when I say museum, I mean museum. Complete with plush red couches too overstuffed to sit on, expensive-looking sculptures that would break if you looked at them funny, and alarms that can go off if you sneeze hard. The place practically screams, "Don't touch me!"

I guess that statement pretty much sums up Max's dad, too. I don't know how Max puts up with those frozen visits every other weekend.

But it was off to the palace with us, no matter what. I was Max's best friend and would not let him suffer alone . . . at least while I could work on getting him to go dive for barrels with me.

Mr. Myer opened the solid oak door with a flourish. "Hi, guys." The greeting would have sounded cheery coming from anyone else's mouth, but Max's dad accomplished sounding distracted and a little disappointed in two words. I got the distinct feeling that he'd forgotten Max was coming . . . and that he'd been expecting someone else.

The wall-to-wall windows across from the door were meant to let in light, but that function was inhibited by the UV coating pasted on them to prevent the "artifacts" from fading.

"What do you guys want to do today?" Mr. Myer's blue eyes looked everywhere but at Max and me. His hands, stuffed in his tattered jeans, jingled loose change.

I opened my mouth to answer, "Go dive," but Max's sharp elbow prevented all but a smothered "oof" from coming out of my mouth.

"Whatever, Dad." Max didn't sound so enthusiastic. His dad's eyes stopped their roaming and landed at his own feet. I almost felt sorry for the guy until I heard his suggestion.

"Let's go sailing."

Yes, it was an outdoor activity. But my idea of an afternoon of fun did not include rocking in a slow back-and-forth motion until I lost track of the horizon and started feeding the fish with my previously eaten lunch. But I'd already endured Max's sharp elbow once and preferred not to get it again. So I didn't say anything as Max agreed, and he and his dad planned the afternoon. Mr. Myer needed to run to the bank and then drop off a few things for his job. In the meantime, Max and I were going to start putting together sack lunches and a few snacks for the boat ride.

It took us all of ten minutes to throw potato chips, sandwiches, grapes, a few bottles of water, and a thermos of juice into the cooler. It was finding the paper plates, napkins, and paper cups that presented a problem. We split up and began scouring the townhouse.

Terrified that I would set off some alarm, I opted for the basement.

I flipped on the light at the top of the stairs and sighed at the sight of a zillion and one boxes, stacked floor to ceiling.

"At least they're all marked," I mumbled to no one. Deciding to just look at a few boxes, I trudged down the steps.

Every box, crate, or package I could see was labeled FRAGILE and marked for delivery to some exotic location around the world—Cambodia, Russia, France, even Morocco. Well, he was in the international imports business. I guess stuff would have to go back and forth.

After hefting a few boxes, I found one with the ever-so-specific label of STUFF. I guess paper plates would be considered "stuff."

I pulled back the tape and started digging through newspaper in the box. It took me a second to realize that it was the *newspaper* being stored. I slowed down, curious as to why Max's dad would keep an entire box full of yellowing newspaper.

All of the cut-up newspaper articles had one thing in common—they were about Max's dad. I sat down and started reading. The top articles in the stack were glowing articles singing the praises of Mr. Myer's work. One was about how he successfully brought well-known artists in to Mr. O'Malley's local gallery. Another was about the security system Mr. Myer had developed. The charities the Myer and O'Malley families had donated huge amounts of money to were the subject of another article. I set all these aside and kept scanning, looking for what had happened to make the two families such enemies.

When I found what I was looking for, I couldn't believe what I read. Mr. Myer had been accused of secretly selling original pieces of art and replacing them with forged copies. The newspaper articles, dating back to just before Max's parents divorced, followed the investigation into Mr. Myer's life. The police had even questioned a known copy artist, Jessica Cumming, who was suspected of helping Mr. Myer.

While their investigation did uncover some rather questionable behavior . . . especially between Jessica and Mr. Myer, the police never had enough evidence to take a case to court. But the suspicion had been enough to hurt the gallery and get Max's dad canned. As I read, it was obvious why there was bad blood between the families.

If the words Mr. O'Malley and Mr. Myer had said were illustrated, it'd be nothing but flames.

I picked up the articles and read them more closely. I studied the clues—the artists' names, the pictures, the captions—and began committing them all to memory. I reached the page mentioning the suspected accomplice—Jessica Cumming—and stopped at the woman's picture. She looked familiar. If I ignored the teased blond hair and concentrated on the sculpted nose, perfect smile, and distinct tilt of her head . . . I could almost make a connection. I chewed on my thumbnail and closed my eyes, trying to put things together.

Janine. It was Janine! My dad's ex-employee who'd skipped work on a whim, preventing dad from diving with us. If she was such an amazing artist, why was she moonlighting as a dive-shop employee? I dug through the clippings and found that she'd been driven out of the art community. Unlike Mr. Myer, she didn't have the connections or the money to start over and no one would hire her as an artist. Apparently the dive shop was the bottom of the barrel.

At that moment I heard the door upstairs shut and the muffled sound of Max and his dad talking. I stuffed the articles back into the box and quickly restacked the boxes. Mr. Myer was just opening the door to the basement when I turned and bounded up the stairs, wearing what I hoped was an innocent look on my face.

As Max and his dad picked up everything for the boat, I stood in the corner trying to think of something to get me out of making the trip.

I didn't know what was going on, but I didn't like it. And I certainly did *not* want to go on an all-day boating trip with someone with this kind of secret.

Unfortunately, my brain remained frozen in shock well into the afternoon, and it wasn't until I had a real emergency, in the form of losing my lunch over the side of Mr. Myer's awful sailboat, the Perfect

Breeze, that I was able to get Max alone. The whole embarrassing scene caused Mr. Myer to call it an afternoon and head in early; he got us back to the dock as quickly as his blow-boat could go.

Despite the fact that the world had yet to stop spinning, I remained sold on the idea that we had to go diving. And that meant not only convincing Max to go dive with me, but our getting up enough guts to go diving on our own. I was more convinced than ever that we were missing something.

As we biked back to my dad's shop, I thought about different ways I might try to convince Max. I decided that being direct was my best option.

We skidded into the dive shop, and I took a deep breath.

"I'll meet you back here at eight. I'm going down to look around with or without you." I'd pulled out the stops. He had to go.

"Diving." I saw his jaw flexing and knew the one word was a challenge. Maybe I'd pushed him too far. He just rolled his eyes and biked away. It wasn't exactly a yes. But it was close.

"See you later," I called after him.

Chapter 10

It was perfect. My mom was taking Suzie, my blond-haired, perfect little sister, out for her traditional "just with Mom" birthday dinner at seven. That was less than an hour away. And Dad would be busy working up front at the shop until it closed at nine, and I knew he was planning on catching up with paperwork after that.

While waiting for Max to come back, I would spend the time helping Dad do whatever needed to be done. It was a good excuse to hang out at the shop.

So far, everything had worked as planned except one small detail: it was 8:30 and Max wasn't at the shop yet.

I turned away from the front window and sulked to the back of the store, where I plopped on the chair behind the counter. Max was never late. This either meant that he'd gotten into some kind of trouble or he'd had enough of me. I decided to check at his house. Maybe he'd still be there.

I grabbed the yellowing counter phone and dialed Max's house. After five rings the machine picked up and I hung up.

Well, I supposed I was on my own. Straightening my shoulders, I walked purposefully to the back storeroom where my dive gear was still stowed in its bag.

"What are you doing?"

I nearly hit the ceiling thinking I'd been busted, but it was just Max.

"I'm going for a dive."

"I can't believe we're doing this."

"We? So you're going?"

"Audrey, don't push it."

I grinned and handed the lift bag to Max.

"I'm only going so that you don't go by yourself and get killed. I'm not carrying these." He handed the hot-air-balloon-shaped bag back to me.

The boat stored in the area behind the equipment room creaked and I stopped cold, looking for an intruder.

I felt like I should have been dressed in black with one of those goofy stocking caps over my ponytail. It wasn't like we were stealing anything, but we were definitely trying not to get caught while taking something that didn't exactly belong to us out of a place of business. However, it proved to be a fairly simple task.

Since our gear bags were still packed in the back, getting them out was easy. Sneak in the back door, grab the black bags, set them outside the door, slip into the back door of the compressor room, swipe two tanks, and tiptoe back out the door. We already had on our swimsuits, so we even avoided having to slip into the bathroom, which you could see from the checkout. Objective one completed.

Next objective: get across the street and down the little ravine to the shore of Lake Michigan without anyone catching on. All that while lugging a good forty pounds of gear apiece. Our training: years of playing hide-and-seek. Our guts proved to be up to the task—so far. Objective two completed.

Those really were the difficult ones, so by the time we were across the street and down the ravine, standing at the edge of the slowly shifting water, I figured we were all set. Behind us we were concealed from view by the hill, on our left by a huge stone break wall, and to the right, by the woods where we'd found the barrel and knife.

We pulled our gear out of the bags. Buoyancy compensator, or BC (the vest thing you wear to help you go up and down in the water); regulator (the thing you breathe through); computer (with the air gauge, compass, and depth meter); lights; fins; boots; mask; snorkel; gloves; and hood (a black hat strangely similar to a ski mask except with the whole face cut out and made of wet-suit material). No need for a dive flag, since we were diving at dusk.

Dusk was the perfect time for this dive. I wanted to dive late enough that there wouldn't be many boats out but early enough so there would be light to see. I definitely wanted to avoid a flat-out night dive. Even though we both had dived at night a million times, we weren't technically certified to do it. But it wasn't the technicality that worried me. I just hated night diving—the silent darkness always made me jumpy, and I was already nervous enough.

Mechanically following the procedures we'd been taught, we put together our gear while automatically checking every piece of equipment for holes or problems. Drop the BC straps over the tank and tighten. Secure the regulator over the valve of the tank. Turn on the tank and computer. Check the air level. Mine read 3100. Check your buddy's. Max's was 3000. Breathe through your main regulator to ensure that it's working. Breathe through the backup. It was a bit tedious for my taste, but this procedure was one thing my dad had successfully drilled into my head.

Then it was time for my least favorite part. Struggling into the dreaded but absolutely necessary wet suit. Not the flimsy suits used by jet skiers and other surface dwellers, these things are at least six millimeters thick, are nearly impossible to get on, and they make you feel like a five-year-old preparing to go outside on a winter's day—arms and legs stiff, and waddling to your destination—but it's 80 degrees outside.

You can see why I despise them. But without a good tight wet suit, the fifty-degree or less water temperature at depth is impossible to withstand for very long. Someone once told me why it felt so cold—something about water removing heat three times faster than air. It doesn't matter much to me. I just know my lips go numb, and I'd prefer that the rest of me not get that way along with them.

I'd just finished maneuvering my wet suit to my waist when I heard a boat engine revving down, as if it were going to stop just off of our little stretch of beach. I dove for my hood to conceal my head—just in case.

It was a long, powerful cigarette boat with flashy yellow and red flames painted up the sides, perfectly complemented by its obnoxiously noisy engines. And it wasn't just the boat that caught my attention. It was the occupants and their actions.

I stood there dumbfounded for what seemed an eternity. I couldn't have described the rest of them well enough for a police sketch artist, but I definitely recognized one guy . . . it was Shawn. But what in the world was he doing? It looked like they were all going to go swimming. Right there in front of us.

All of a sudden my mind snapped back to more immediate concerns. We were going to be busted. I opened my hood and yanked it over my head, managing to pull out more than one strand of hair by the roots in the process. I turned to see that Max already had his on. A look of utter disbelief registered on his face.

The boat turned its bow toward shore and slowly motored in. I think Max could hear my heart pounding, because he swiveled to face me, shooting a withering look my way. I swallowed hard, thinking of excuses: "We were just going swimming." "My dad's on his way." But they all fell flat.

And then, the miracle. The captain turned the boat south, revved its engines, and took off. Max and I stood there for several moments, until sweat dripped into my eyes, reminding me that we were still standing there like stiff-limbed kids decked out in our winter wear.

"That was close." I had such a grasp of the obvious. I had no idea what Shawn and his friends were doing, but I was thrilled that we'd escaped notice. I was trying to convince myself that his showing up and then leaving was a sign that it was okay for us to dive by ourselves.

But I didn't want to think much on what all this implied about Shawn—why he was on the large, fast, expensive boat as it stopped in front of the little area of beach where we'd found the barrel. Lake Michigan was a huge lake with hundreds of miles of shoreline. What were the possibilities of this being mere chance? No matter what I thought about him, Shawn was Max's brother, and if he was one of the burglars . . . well, I didn't want to think about it. I forced myself to move, and turned to Max.

"Here, tuck in my hood for me."

Max stood gaping at me for a moment, then tucked the skirt of my hood into my wet suit and zipped it up the rest of the way. I repeated the process on him. Then I helped him into his BC and he helped me—one arm at a time. With most of our gear on, we both double-checked our computers and regulators and eased into the water.

Walking out to chest height, we carried our fins, gloves, and heavy-duty dive lights. This was often the most frustrating part of gearing up. As I tried to maintain a grip on two gloves and one fin, I leaned over to attempt to fasten the other fin to my foot, all the while making sure that the waves that were constantly beating against me didn't knock me over. A face plant into the water, though cooling, was not an impressive diver move.

Max, as usual, accomplished the entire task before I had successfully clicked a single clasp into the designated slot.

Max took my two gloves and my other fin and stood bracing me against the waves, while I continued my struggle. I finally heard the satisfying click. The other fin went on without a hitch. Impatient with myself, I wrestled on my now soaking-wet gloves—brrr!—and yanked my mask into place. I signaled the international three-finger-up sign for OK and received the OK response. Max signaled down with his thumb and I signaled back.

Holding up the tube that dumped the air out of my BC, I pressed a button and heard the hissing that indicated the air escaping from my vest. I lay down in the water, plugged my nose, and blew gently to equalize the pressure in my ears to the added pressure of the water. We slowly finned forward, dropping with the contour of the lake bottom beneath us.

Diving is one of my favorite things in the world to do, and this dive quickly made me forget about Shawn and the burglars.

It was absolutely peaceful. The sounds from the surface were deadened to a whisper. My body was almost weightless. On a clear day in northern Lake Michigan you could see crystal-blue water forever—a perfect dream world. God certainly knew what he was doing when he created this second world beneath the forbidding surface of the water.

As we descended lower, the temperature of the water dropped, numbing my still-broken lip and making me glad I'd struggled into my wet suit. I swam forward on my stomach, looking at the huge rocks beneath me. Letting the current and slow kicks carry me forward, I watched little crawdads closing and opening their claws in warning as they swished around the silently swaying algae peaks. I was staring down one particularly haughty crawfish, when I looked up and spotted a rock jutting out in front of me. I inhaled deeply, inflating my lungs like a balloon to rise above the rock. That was close. Too close. Breathing hard, I struggled to regain the calm I usually achieved easily on a dive.

That reminded me to check my depth gauge. Thirty-five feet. We had decided before the dive that we'd start our search pattern at forty feet. We were doing a U search pattern. We'd swim for a predetermined number of kicks straight out—thirty for today. Then we would take a ninety-degree turn and swim parallel to shore for about ten strokes before turning back to shore for our thirty strokes, followed by another turn to run parallel to shore. We'd repeat the pattern until we ran low on air or we found whatever it was we were looking for. I focused on the pattern and forced myself to breathe slowly, calmly.

On our first pass, we hit a pretty steep drop-off about twenty-five kicks out. A strange clicking noise made me jump and spin in a frantic circle, and I nearly collided with Max.

He grinned around his regulator and showed me that the noise was him banging on his tank. Once I'd calmed down a bit, he started scribbling on his dive slate. "Turn now. Drop last five kicks."

I nodded and signed OK. Despite the water clarity, it was theoretically possible to hide a barrel in the rock-strewn shallows. So we'd stick to the shallower area . . . for now.

To keep focused on searching the bottom, I noted on my slate each fish illuminated by my dive light—a bass, a few red and white blennies. I would later record this information, along with my depth and bottom-time stats, in my private dive log.

For a moment I flipped onto my back to look at the surface, relaxing my breathing again. Though visibility was a little low, I could still see the surface rippling and shimmering in the setting sun. It reminded me of the pictures on my dad's wall. The sparkling surface of Lake Michigan looked identical to the Caribbean.

I heard the low rumble of a boat somewhere nearby, the sound growing louder. It was heading closer to us, but since we were far below the surface of the water, I wasn't concerned.

I flipped back into a swimmer's crawl position to move up and over another pile of rocks. I checked my gauges: seventy-five feet. Catching Max's eye, I pointed to my computer and then held up five fingers on my right hand and two on my left: 700 psi of air left. Enough for one more pass. He signaled OK.

We turned to head back to shore, when I heard several odd splashes followed by the hard revving of an engine. It was dark enough that no boat should be going fast enough to create a wake. I looked up to the surface to see if I could see what was going on, but in flipping over I'd stirred up the sand on the bottom and seriously diminished our visibility. I turned to my right to check on Max. He wasn't in his normal position. I whipped to my left.

I couldn't find him. It was my dream. My nightmare. Why had I gone on this dive?

I looked down at my dive computer to start the countdown. And tried to control my breathing while I looked around again. Left. Right. Up. Down. Turn 180 degrees and repeat. I saw bubbles to my left, and blue fins bobbing strangely in the water.

Max was a good twenty or more fin strokes behind me and he was fine. He was looking at a black drum shooting down to the bottom. As I watched, Max smoothly pushed against the water in front of him to move backward, out of the way of the drums. I was curious as well, but didn't want to risk getting caught in the ropes trailing the barrels to the floor of the lake. Suddenly, Max's body snapped back and I saw that one of the ropes had snaked around his leg and had caught it tight.

"Max!" My scream was muffled in the water and I choked on the water I'd let into my mouth.

As Max struggled to free himself, I frantically finned back to him, pulling my dive knife from the holder on my BC. His eyes were wide as he was dragged down toward the drop-off. His body landed on the rocks I had just avoided, and he flung his arms around the nearest one to avoid being pulled into the black depths behind him. But the drums, heavy with their contents, sped downward.

Just as I reached Max, the rope tightened around his leg and I heard an awful snap accompanied by a muffled scream. Max was barely holding on.

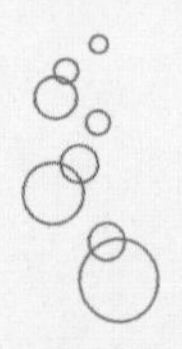

Chapter 11

Breathe. Just breathe. I didn't know if my thought commands were for him or for me as I sawed through the yellow line. My nightmare had become real.

By the time I'd finally cut through the line I couldn't hear Max's breathing bubbles. Grasping his shoulders, I looked into his eyes. He was conscious, but his eyes were already glazing. I wasn't a certified rescue diver, but every diver is trained for basic emergencies and my father had drilled me well.

I touched his goggles with my fingers and then touched mine—*Look at me.*

I purposefully exhaled and then pointed to him. He exhaled, then inhaled, and nodded. I checked my pressure gauge. Down to 200 psi. Max had the same. To be safe, most divers tried to surface with 500 psi—we'd have to skip our safety stop, and risk breaking the deco limits and getting bent. I dumped the air out of his BC to prevent us from shooting upward at the surface when the air began to expand.

Flipping on my side, I wrapped my arms around Max's chest and began frog kicking. I forced myself to slow my breathing, forced the panic back down to my stomach, and began to rise with painful slowness to the surface and the beach . . . all Max needed was for me to rush to the surface too quickly, producing a bubble of air in his spine. We needed to breathe off as much of the excess air and nitrogen as we could on our way to dry land.

As soon as I broke the surface, I inflated Max's BC and flipped him onto his back. Spitting my regulator out of my mouth, I yanked off my fins and mask, grabbed Max by the shoulders, and dragged him free of the waves. I wiggled out of my BC and turned to Max. I hadn't been trained in rescue diving, but I had to try to make sure he was okay.

As I peeled off his BC and tank, Max's eyes rolled back in pain. His face had turned a sickly shade of khaki, almost the color of the sand . . . and it was my fault.

I had to keep him warm. For the first time, I looked up to see where we were and to try and figure out what to do. I hadn't been following my compass on the return trip, and the current had dumped us farther down shore than I'd expected. The abandoned cottages in front of us were stark against the quickly darkening sky. I shivered and turned to look back down the beach. I couldn't see our gear bags, but they had to be there. I needed to get our towels to keep Max warm.

I ran down the beach, slipping in the sand, scanning for our bags. I found them tucked neatly in the underbrush, right where we'd left them. I grabbed the bags and sprinted back to Max.

Dropping to my knees, I unzipped our gear bags. "Open your eyes, Max. You have to stay awake." My hands shook as I pulled our towels out of the bags.

Knowing his wet suit would only make him colder, I unzipped it and worked it down to his waist, then wrapped him in our matching towels.

"I'm going for help." He just nodded and blinked blindly at me. Grabbing his face in my hands, I looked directly into his eyes. "Max, listen to me. Max!" His eyes spun as he tried to focus. "You have to stay awake, Max."

"You already said that." He grinned weakly.

Always joking. "Max, this isn't funny." But at least I knew he was still processing what I was saying.

"I know. Just go get your dad and stop standing there like a post."

I spun back around toward the road. I didn't want to leave him but didn't have a choice. I ran away from the lake and my friend, dodging between cars, their lights blurring in front of me.

My lungs burned, but I forced my legs to keep moving. The red-lettered dive shop sign had never been so welcome—or so far away.

The little electronic bell signaled my entry a moment before "Dad!" escaped my lips.

"Dad, Max is hurt!"

Weaving between the wet suits, tanks, and other equipment up front, I ran to the back of the store, bursting through the office door just next to the fill room.

"Dad."

He was on the phone and held up a finger without even looking up.

Ignoring him, I started in again. "Dad, Max is hurt. We need the emergency oxygen and the hypothermia blankets, and you have to call 9-1-1."

That got his attention, and he looked up at me, dripping in his doorway. His expression morphed from bored to shocked, then to scared.

At first it seemed as though we were both in one of those old movies where everything goes really slow while the bullet flies through the air or the car jumps the cliff. But then Dad shoved the phone into my hand, telling me to call the ambulance, and I struggled to tell him where Max was. He ran through the back door of his office and into the equipment room. His footsteps thundered out of the shop. I heard his voice through my mental fog, telling me to stay put and watch the shop. The front door sensor beeped, and the door swung closed.

"Hello?" The voice on the phone pulled me back to my task.

"We've, um . . . we've had an emergency. Mr. Barrister went for help. Would you call back later?"

Not waiting for a response, I hung up the phone and dialed 9-1-1. The woman on the phone told me I was brave to be so calm as I told her what had happened and where Max was. I knew she was asking more questions. I didn't answer. I couldn't. She said something about the paramedics coming and I pushed a button, cutting the woman off in mid-sentence.

The door sensor beeped again. The phone started its off-the-hook tone. The wood paneling behind Dad's desk blurred.

I'd gotten Max hurt and was standing in the dive shop in my dripping wet suit, a testimony to the fact that I'd lied, disobeyed my parents, and put Max in serious danger. I dropped the phone, letting it swing free, and slumped to the floor, leaning against Dad's creaky old metal desk. I watched as the water from my hair dripped, puddling on the gray linoleum.

There was nothing I could do to help the paramedics or my dad, and I couldn't face what I'd done. The adults would take care of Max. They would do the right thing.

The right thing. You'd think I could stumble on it once in a while.

I didn't know what to pray, so I didn't. I didn't know what to think, so I didn't. Staring at the wall in front of me, I fell into a mind-numbing trance.

I don't know how long I sat there, but it had to have been awhile. It was completely dark out when I finally stood, shivering and damp.

I pulled my hood off, struggled out of my wet suit, washed them out in the rinse tank, and hung everything to drip dry in the back room. I couldn't bear to go back to the beach to get the rest of the equipment. I didn't want to see where my friend had been . . . or think about what could have happened.

Digging my street clothes out of my locker, I stumbled to the bathroom and changed out of my bathing suit.

Looking in the mirror, I shook my head. I looked the part of an irresponsible bonehead: worn-out, torn jean shorts and wrinkled T-shirt; eyes rimmed in red (the right one with a bruise in full bloom below it); cheeks splotched from cold and fear. My hair hung loosely from the ponytail holder on the top of my head, sticking up at odd angles and places. And to top it all off, a split lip.

Mrs. Myer had made it clear that we needed to let the professionals do their job. I had learned my lesson. No more Sherlock Holmes for me . . . and that was a promise.

Chapter 12

That night I couldn't sleep. I sat on my blue-and-yellow-striped bedspread and stared at my tall wood dresser across the room, the scene with my dad replaying over and over in my head.

I was sitting in his office, breathing from the oxygen tank . . . just to be safe. And dad was leaning against the wall. His eyes had lost their sparkle.

"Audrey, you know better than to dive by yourself. You know how dangerous diving can be. What were you thinking?"

I'd wanted to be the hero. I'd wanted to be like Mrs. Myer, the one to save the city from a rash of burglaries . . . to be famous for breaking the story. But none of that mattered to me. Not anymore. I'd disobeyed my dad and almost gotten my best friend killed in the process.

"I don't know. We were looking for clues. It was dumb. I don't know."

"Well, you *do* know you're grounded. I don't know for how long yet. I'll be able to process more once we hear what the doctors have to say about Max and his recovery. I'll let you go to the hospital to see Max, but other than that, you are homebound. And you *will* help your mom out around the house without a word of complaint. I never expected this from you, Audrey."

I think his words were punishment enough. And go to the hospital?

Even if his mom were willing to let me near him, Max probably would never want to see me again.

In the early morning I finally fell asleep and was awakened by the sounds of my little sister singing in the shower, and by a beam of sunshine that had sneaked around my blinds, glaring in at me, ready to expose me for the kind of person I really was. I lay staring at my ceiling until my mom quietly knocked and reminded me that it was Sunday and I needed to get ready for church. I tried to ignore the obnoxiously cheery sunshine, but it was persistent and made the throbbing in my head ten times worse.

I stumbled out of bed and headed across the hallway to the bathroom that I share with my sister. Suzie, the perfect wonder, was already standing in front of the mirror brushing her teeth. Though she hadn't done anything with her golden blond locks yet, her hair cascaded down her back in perfect little wet ringlets. She was a mirror image of Mom. A petite Dutch beauty. The exact opposite of me.

Suzie caught me looking at her and stuck her tongue out. If I thought I could get away with it, I might have belted her. I made do with a low growl and a menacing look before I turned on the shower and got ready for church. Sunday was the one day of the week that I wore a dress, at Mom's insistence. At times I felt like one of her porcelain dolls, ready to be dressed up with the frilly lace and occasional pink bow in my hair.

But today I wore the only dress I really liked—the navy blue one with big impressionistic flowers scattered across it—and pulled my dark hair back into a ponytail. Strictly functional, but it was all I was capable of today. If I had to go to church and face God, the one being who'd be more disappointed in me than my dad was the day after I'd nearly killed my best friend, at least I'd be comfortable.

My mom walked around the corner just as I was leaving the bathroom and gasped, grabbing my cheeks in her iron grip.

"I can't believe you. Look at your face. It's awful. What will the pastor think?"

That was the last thing I was worried about. Even if Pastor James could focus on my face through his wrist-thick glasses from one hundred paces, I don't think my fat lip would change his opinion of me. He was one of the few adults in the church who would run around behind the church with the little kids, playing hide-and-seek. I'd even seen him roll down the hill on the side yard like a sausage.

He'd more likely be concerned about my lying, disobedient soul that was sure to rot in hell after yesterday. But I endured Mom's ranting with sealed lips. There was no point in arguing with her, so I just made my way downstairs.

Dad and Suzie were already eating their cereal at the table. Mom poured me some, and I ate a few bites to make her happy. Trying to avoid the sadness in my dad's eyes, I finally just dropped my bowl in the sink and made my way out to the old Subaru Outback.

It was a relief to arrive at church and escape the quiet awkwardness in the car.

My favorite part of the service, the singing, was in full swing, and I joined in halfheartedly, trying to stop thinking about Max. He was supposed to have come to church with us today, and he loved to sing, too. I swiped angrily at the moisture hanging onto my eyelashes. I would not feel sorry for myself. I didn't need to cry in church.

We sat when one of the men sitting on the platform walked to the podium with his Bible and signaled for us to sit. He gently placed his Bible on top of the wooden pulpit, adjusted his glasses, and began reading.

> Truthful lips endure forever, but a lying tongue lasts only a moment. There is deceit in the hearts of those who plot evil, but joy for those who promote peace. No harm befalls the

> righteous, but the wicked have their fill of trouble. The LORD detests lying lips, but he delights in men who are truthful. (Proverbs 12:19–22)

I slunk low in my seat, trying to avoid eye contact with the man on the platform, and desperately hoping my parents and Pastor James wouldn't be able to see me. I didn't want to see the judgment in their faces.

"The LORD detests lying lips." I stared straight at the burgundy carpet and counted the specks of gray thread I saw there.

The Lord hates lying lips and I . . . I was the biggest liar ever to walk the earth.

Before I knew it, the service was over. My mind had been so busy working through the Bible passage for the day, I had barely heard Pastor James. God couldn't really detest me, could he?

At the final amen, I bolted. I successfully avoided my parents, but Suzie cornered me in the back of the auditorium. Her look said it all: *God's gonna throw a lightning bolt down on you and take you out.* Suzie grinned, smug in her holy perfection.

I turned and trudged down the stairs, heading toward my classroom. Sunday school was actually a pretty cool place. And most days I didn't mind going, but I didn't want to deal with anyone today. I just wanted Max to be okay, and since that wasn't possible, I wanted to be at home where I could sulk.

Weaving through the little kids hanging on to their parents and the older high school kids, I swung around the corner, right into the path of my not-so-best-friend Lucas.

"Hey, look, it's the little Jap lover."

Maybe it was because I didn't remember Lucas being quite so short . . . which I later realized was because I usually saw him from ground level, just after he'd helped me to a "seat." And I guess I forgot how much the whole knife incident had scared me, because the next thing I knew, I was opening my big mouth.

"Lucas, are you really so stupid that you can't even get your insults right? He's Cambodian, brainiac."

It did stop his mouth, but not his fist. I ducked his first swipe and landed one of my own under his chin. But his other fist planted itself squarely across my jaw. I don't remember anything after that until I heard my mom's voice and came to with a jolt of cold from a wet paper towel.

"I don't think you will ever live up to your namesake. Audrey Hepburn had such carriage."

I closed my eyes quickly. My head hurt.

"Audrey, pumkin', lay still. Jill said you hit the back of your head on the wall on the way down. You may have a concussion."

"Great," I said . . . or at least tried to say. Somehow my voice wasn't quite working. I supposed that was okay. It had only been getting me into trouble lately.

I cracked my eyes open cautiously, looking around. My dad, who was holding my hand, was talking seriously with my mom and Jill, one of the youth-group workers. Lucas sat in a corner, arms crossed and eyes closed. But a small bruise was developing on his chin. At least I landed one good hit, though I'm not sure my mom would recognize the "good" in that.

"What happened?" It was Dad's question. I was awake now, and Dad was scoping out the situation, his fist clenching and releasing, clenching and releasing. I hoped Dad's anger was directed toward Lucas, but I hadn't yet ruled out being dead meat myself.

"I'm not really sure," said Sarah, one of the few leaders who could see the horns that held up Lucas's halo. "From what the other kids say, Lucas egged Audrey on by saying something about her being a 'Jap lover.' Next thing I know, they're throwing punches, she's on the floor, and I'm talking to Lucas. Lucas has never been a stellar example in this class, but this really is over the top, even for him."

"That would explain why Audrey flipped," Dad said. "Her best friend, who is Asian, was just injured quite badly." He sat there, squeezing the bridge of his nose between his thumb and forefinger—a sure sign of a headache and more trouble for me. "I know that doesn't excuse her actions, but it does help explain things." His voice dropped at the end of the sentence and he looked at me. His eyes were tired and sad.

I'd disappointed him. Again.

Chapter 13

I was, according to my mom, grounded for life. But it didn't matter. God had certainly sent *his* message on a flashing neon sign big enough for everyone to see: *Audrey Barringer, a liar and horrible person, is forever banned from me.*

I'd not only disappointed my mom and dad again, but God, too. The words I'd heard in church echoed in my head, "The LORD detests . . ." There'd be no escaping his judgment.

It was Monday, the day after those fateful words were read in the church's pulpit. As I struggled to wake from a restless sleep, I could see that the sun already had stretched well above the horizon. I could hear Suzie plunking quietly on the piano in the basement. Practicing. Something my folks always had to force me to do. But not anymore.

I was a new kid. No more exploring. No more complaints. No more trouble. I was going to make Mom and Dad proud that I was their child, even if it meant wearing a dress like the other girls at school.

Rolling out of bed, I cringed at the stiffness in my neck and shoulders but found my way into the bathroom to shower. I let the warm water ease the knots in my back, and quickly washed up. Turning off the water, I wrapped myself in a towel and grabbed the brush to pull through my hair.

I looked up into the mirror. The girl's eyes were shimmering.

I blinked.

A wet drop trailed down her cheek. Swiping it away, I stalked across the hallway to my room and into my closet.

I started my new life clean and in nice khaki shorts and a shirt my mom had bought me—white with a big sunflower. Decidedly girly, but perfect for the new me. A glance in the mirror behind my door revealed someone I wasn't familiar with but could get used to.

Before I went downstairs, I made my bed, cleaned my room, and grabbed the laundry. If I was going to be stuck at home for the next few days, I might as well make myself useful.

Lugging the basket down the narrow staircase, I narrowly missed knocking Suzie in the head.

Knowing that I couldn't do much to prevent her from doing it, she slipped under the basket and around me, and pinched the back of my leg.

I screeched, dropped the basket, and stood like an idiot, watching the white basket tumble end over end. In slow motion, the clothes distributed themselves in clumps here and there down the cream-colored stairs.

Before I knew what I was doing, I was screaming at the top of my lungs as I turned and pumped my legs, launching my body back up the stairs. It was a life and death chase. Suzie was going to die.

It was the voice of my mom echoing off the stairwell walls that made me stop short.

"Audrey Marie Barringer!"

So much for my being a new person.

"But, Mom . . ."

"Don't you but me. Apologize to your sister and clean up this mess!"

I will be nice. I will be nice.

"Yes, ma'am."

She turned to wade down the stairs through the clothes, just before Suzie poked her head out the bedroom door and stuck her tongue out at me.

I will be nice.

Taking a deep breath, I gathered the laundry basket and clothes and made my way down to the laundry room in the basement.

Whipping open the washing machine lid, I smashed the clothes in. Socks. T-shirts. Dad's white work shirts. Flipping the dial, I turned the machine on, poured in the detergent, and slammed the lid.

This was going to be harder than I had thought.

I leaned my head back against the doorframe. *Lord, I know you're probably not talking to me right now. I don't even know if you're listening. But if you want me to be different, you're going to have to help. I'm not very good at this.*

What to do next? I spied a likely candidate—the overflowing basket of clean laundry on the floor, the "to iron" pile. I plugged in the iron and dug in.

"Audrey."

I couldn't tell from the tone of her voice whether I was in more trouble or if Mom was just confused.

"I'm down here," I called out musically in my new sweet voice.

"Breakfast is ready."

"Thanks, Mom." Unlike my old self, I ran immediately up the stairs so Mom wouldn't have to ask a second time.

"This smells great."

"What were you doing downstairs?"

"Laundry."

"You're not getting out of your grounding." Why was Mom being so suspicious?

"I know. I'm just trying to help." I could tell she didn't believe me.

I started to try and explain, but Suzie swept into the room, and Mom busied herself with making up Suzie's plate of pancakes.

For four hours I scrubbed, wiped, vacuumed, and generally made myself helpful. At every turn Suzie was there, egging me on. I just ignored her. The weird thing is that after a few hours of Suzie's harassment, Mom busted her and sent her out to work in the yard. I guess Mom isn't blind after all. I was scrubbing the brown crud from the stove in the kitchen when Mom came in behind me and handed me a glass of juice.

"Thanks for your help, Audrey. Why don't you go to the dive shop and help your dad out for a while? You'll enjoy that more than working here, and your dad could really use your help with Mr. Broome gone."

What was that I heard? The call of freedom? I barely kept my cheers of joy inside and managed an unenthusiastic "Okay" instead.

"I'll drive you down there." Okay, it was partial freedom. But it was better than ironing all day. I dropped my glass in the dishwasher and ran downstairs to unplug the iron.

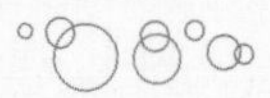

At the shop, Mom dropped me off at the side door. She was waving at me as a red convertible cautiously turned right out of the front entrance and onto the street.

I don't think Mom saw the car. However, this time I was *certain* it was Mr. Broome's car—the personalized "Diver2" plate told me that. But I couldn't tell if it was Mr. Broome. The person looked a bit smaller and thinner than Mr. Broome but was wearing Mr. Broome's classic baseball cap. I frowned, trying to figure out what was going on.

Mom's voice broke into my thoughts. "Just call me on the cell if you need me to come pick you up."

I gave her a quick wave and pushed open the back door. The lights were out again in the back room. There was a slit of light coming out from under Dad's office door. Halfway across the room, it joined the dim light from the archway to the store. Dad never had the lights off out back, and this was the second time in two days. It was weird. A shadow crossed in front of me, sending me back out the door.

Gulping, I willed the rock out of my stomach and stretched my arm around the doorframe, feeling for the light switch just inside and to the left of the doorframe. The overhead lights up between the metal rafters flickered and blinked on. I laughed at the wet suit just inside the door, swaying in the breeze. I was freaking out for nothing.

I stood for a moment more, trying to stop my pounding heart. *I am a wimp!*

Dad's muffled voice came from behind his office door. I decided to let him know I was here and ask what I could do to help.

Remembering my new manners, I quietly knocked and pushed the door open a crack. The overhead light was off but Dad's desktop light was on, creating a shaky, odd silhouette of Dad's profile against the right wall.

His phone was tucked carefully under his ear.

"Sorry," I whispered and began pulling the door shut.

"Au!" Then I heard the beeping on the phone; it'd been off the hook for a while.

"Dad!" I ran to his side. Silver duct tape wound around his arms and torso, and anchored him to the chair back. His legs were similarly bound to the chair's legs. His mouth was taped shut. The strong blue eyes I'd always depended on showed a strange mix of fear and courage.

I stood still for a moment, unsure of what to do. *Move, Audrey!*

My thoughts jarred me to action. I ripped the tape off Dad's mouth and began clawing at the tape around his hands.

"Your pocketknife, Audrey." *Ah yes, my ever-present little knife. I was so dependable in a crisis!*

Frantically I dug the knife out of my pocket and carefully cut his arms free and then his legs. Dad put his hands on the desk and pushed himself to his feet.

"Are you okay?" I realized with surprise that it was my voice asking the question.

"Audrey, you need to get out of here. They might come back." He pulled me to his chest and quickly released me.

"They're gone, Dad."

"How do you know?"

"If they were still in the back room when I got here, they would have . . ." I gulped. "They would have . . ." I was suddenly at a loss for words.

The police were there for hours. Talking to Dad. Then to me. Then Dad. Then me again.

I finally told the one with the dusty blond hair and "J. VanderVeen" on his gold-colored name tag, about the lock pick I'd found. They wanted to know why I hadn't told anyone before. Since I didn't have a good answer, I didn't say anything.

"Show it to me then."

I dug through the dive gloves. A panic started forming in my stomach. I dug through the boots in the next cubby. Then the regulator bin. It was gone. The thief had come back to remove the stuff. Dad must have caught him in the back room where he didn't belong.

"Gone?" he asked. I hadn't realized I'd announced my discovery out loud. I let the tears squeezing out of my eyes answer his question.

I had thought the questions were tough before. But now, the police wanted to know everything. I heard myself telling them about the dive incident, about seeing Mr. Broome's car around town, the knife in Shawn's jeans, even the cigarette boat near the woods.

At this point I just wanted to go home.

Home. It didn't seem as much a prison as it had just a short time ago.

I was sitting slumped against the wall outside Dad's office when I heard Mom's voice calling for me.

"Mom?" She ran around the corner, her skirt brushing the door as she came into the office. Her arms wrapped around me—tight. "Mom." I was so scared; it was all I could manage as I blinked back the tears blurring my vision.

"It's okay, sweetheart." She kneeled in front of me, one arm around my back, the other stroking my head on her shoulder. "You're okay."

Officer VanderVeen peered around the corner. "You're free to go. But, Audrey, be careful, and if you see anything else, call me immediately." His head disappeared around the corner, but I could still hear his voice through the poorly insulated walls.

"Chief, I'm a little concerned about letting Audrey go. She knows quite a lot, and the burglars are getting dangerous enough that—" His voice grew silent as he evidently listened to a response from the chief. "Okay," the officer continued. "I'll have Snyder tail her for a while, just to make sure."

I didn't want any of this to be happening. I didn't want Mr. Broome or Max's brother to be involved.

Then I remembered Lucas's new bike. "Officer. Officer! There's one more thing." And I told him about Lucas's new bike and how I'd seen him at the dive shop just before coming in. Maybe it had been Lucas. He could have planted the knife in Shawn's jeans at the park, or maybe Shawn picked it up there. One of the guys definitely *did* have a knife. And Lucas obviously had come into some money. And he'd been here. My words were tumbling over one another. It was the answer.

"It wasn't Lucas, but thanks for the information. I'm glad you're telling me everything now." He was trying to be nice to not make me feel like an idiot.

But, why? Why was the officer so sure it wasn't Lucas? It was obvious to me that Lucas was capable of something like this. He'd rearranged my face a few times, hadn't he? Why was it impossible that he was involved?

I looked at Mom and she just shook her head.

"Let's go home, sweetheart." Mom was standing now, offering her hand. She was right. I'd just seen my dad tied up and the officer was worried about me. I did not need to go investigate. *Won't I ever learn?* I couldn't stop the tears again. This was all my fault.

I just needed to talk to someone who would understand. Mom and Dad loved me. I knew that, but they didn't always understand. Max. I needed him and hoped he'd forgive me. "Mom, I want to see Max." I hiccupped. "Can I go see him?"

"Sure, honey. I'll take you."

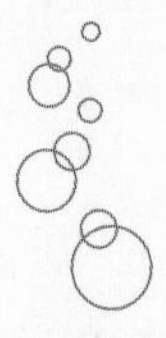

Chapter 14

The hospital doors swished open, cool, air-conditioned air sweeping out the door. I waved to Officer Snyder, who sat calmly in his blue-and-white cop car. He grinned at me and waved as he settled in to wait for me.

Port Haven General Hospital is nothing like the hospitals you see on TV—at least not the front entrance. Instead of white tile and faded green walls, it has classy dark woods and patterned carpet. I suppose they were meant to impress the wealthy patrons who came from miles around for care.

My dirty tennis shoes contrasted with the posh surroundings and left little marks here and there as I approached the massive desk and the hospital attendant sitting there, dispensing information.

A piece of paper with the neat handwriting of the professional-looking attendant told me to go to the south elevator bank just around the corner, get off at the fifth floor, and then turn left. If I got lost, it said, I was to ask for help at the nurses' station.

The elevator bell rang cheerily, and I stepped into the middle elevator. I listened to the sound of electricity and pulleys humming as the car rose. The little numbers lit and faded in sequence: 2, 3, 4. Bouncing a bit, the elevator stopped, the number 5 glowing brightly. Fifth floor.

Swallowing hard, I waited as the doors opened and quickly escaped the too bright box . . . stepping directly into Lucas. *He's going to kill me. He knows I know about him.*

"Watch where you're going, twit," he said. I cringed, waiting for the fist to rearrange my face for the third time in just a few days. But he just shouldered past me and walked down the hall.

I released my breath and glanced at the moist sheet of paper in my hands, then looked down the corridor where it told me to go—the same direction Lucas had just headed. The other direction was the nurses' station. Maybe someone there would take me to Max's room and protect me from Lucas. I headed that way.

Up here, the hospital looked a little bit more like those on TV. The white tile glared at me as I trudged to the gleaming counter. There was a mass of activity behind the counter. I didn't know what to do, so I stood there, numbly waiting for someone to notice me.

"Audrey?"

The sound came from behind me. Somehow it didn't quite register.

"Audrey?"

It was the gentle touch on my shoulder that jerked me back to reality. It was Amy O'Malley—Lucas's younger sister, who was a year behind me in school.

"Audrey, what are you doing here?" Amy's eyebrows crunched together in concern.

Even though Amy's blond hair and blue eyes made her look like she belonged to her family, she had somehow escaped the obnoxious nature of the rest of the O'Malley clan. She was always the one on the playground who would be wiping away tears from the little kids' cheeks when they were hurt. Everyone liked Amy. Right now, she was really and truly concerned about me.

"Max was hurt in a diving accident," I mumbled. Her eyebrows arched but she didn't say anything. "We were looking for a submerged barrel." And suddenly I was telling her the whole story. The lock picks. The knife. The connection to the burglars.

I was halfway through my tale when I looked up and realized that Amy was sobbing, her face buried in her hands.

Chapter 15

"Amy?" I apparently had a knack today for hurting people. "Amy?" I asked again.

It was my turn to be concerned. Her hands fell away from her face and her hair draped forward, revealing a huge bruise on the back of her neck. I looked down at her wrist to see another set on the insides of her wrists.

"Amy, what in the world?"

"They robbed our house last night."

"They . . . what? Who?" I stood staring at her, unable to process what she was saying.

"The burglars. They came in from the back of the house by the lake. There were three of them." She glanced up at me, her fair skin stained with tears. And here I was thinking her brother was one of them. The officer would have known about the break-in. *I am such an idiot.*

I forced a tight smile and grabbed her hand.

I'm sure she'd already been forced to relate the story to the cops. But they weren't Amy's friends. So I listened, barely breathing.

They had used a speedboat to get onto the back side of the property that bordered the lake, and had sneaked in through the back door while the family was watching a movie.

They all had guns and were talking to each other in a language Amy didn't understand. She thought maybe Asian.

Asian? My mind was whirling. *Asian?*

Lord in heaven. Please, no, Lord. There were very few people I knew who actually spoke an Asian language. And they all were connected to Max's family or Mr. Broome. *What do I do now, Lord?*

Amy handed me a tissue. I hadn't realized that I'd been crying.

"My dad's still in surgery. He was . . . he was trying to protect me. I don't think they would have hurt us, but he didn't want them to tie us up. So they, uh . . ." The tears came again and I knew. I knew they'd shot Mr. O'Malley. I clenched my fists. *How could they?*

Mrs. Myer was right. They were getting more dangerous.

"Amy, everything will be okay. The doctors here are amazing. They'll help him." I didn't know what else to say.

She smiled at me as if I had said something profound.

"I just hope they find those men," I said and smiled as she sniffled.

"Me, too. Tell Max I'm praying for him." And with that, she moved back down the hall.

My mind was whirling. There had to be something I could do. But I had told the cops what I knew, and I wasn't going to go investigate. So there was nothing else I could do but wait and pray. *Lord God, please help the cops find the burglars before this gets any worse. Please, God, help me know what to do and say.*

I turned and walked down the hall toward Max's room.

I hesitated in front of the solid wood door. Would Max even want to see me? I raised my hand to knock when the door opened and a nurse strode out. I stepped out of her way and grabbed the door before it closed. It was now or never.

I peered around the corner. "Max?"

He was there, his head bandaged and his leg stiff and hanging from a contraption above his bed. His face was pale, but he smiled.

"You look awful, Audrey." Always the humor.

I smiled. "I'm glad you're okay. I was really worried. I'm sorry—sorry for everything." I clamped my mouth shut to stop the flow.

"Your dad took great care of me, but I'm guessing you're grounded for, what, life?" His knowing smile lit up his eyes.

"Something like that."

"Audrey, you've been my best friend since we were little, but I've got to tell you, you know how to get in trouble better than anyone I know."

"It's not like I try," I hedged.

"Um . . . let's see. You purposefully disobeyed your parents, not to mention my mom, and lied to how many people?"

I opened my mouth to argue, but he was right. I dropped into the chair next to his bed. "I know. I'm a screw-up. But I really have been trying. I . . ." Dissolving into dripping tears was not a normal thing for me to do, but I found myself a shaking mass of tears for what seemed like the fiftieth time that day. "I'm so sorry, Max. I really am." I stood to leave. I couldn't do this. I couldn't take the embarrassment anymore, or the guilt.

"Audrey, I didn't mean to make you cry. I chose to go with you. This was my fault, too."

"It's okay. I deserve it."

"Hey, if you want to make it up to me, will you read to me for a bit? These meds have me so messed up, I can't see straight enough to watch TV, let alone read." He pointed to the book by the side of the bed, *Twenty Thousand Leagues Under the Sea.* Appropriate, I guess.

So I sat and read until I heard Max's breathing fall into steady rasps. I set the book down and looked at my friend. He had bed-head—his hair was bent into the shape of a wing where it had been pressed into the pillows—but his sheets were perfectly crisp and folded neatly under his arms. I smiled. Only Max could look nearly perfect in the hospital.

I thought about the last few days and everything that had happened. Pulling my knees up to my chest, I lay my head down, cradling myself in the armchair.

The barrel! How could I be so stupid? I forgot to tell the officer about the barrels that were dropped on us. Officer Snyder. I had to talk to Officer Snyder.

I scribbled a somewhat legible note to Max and left it for him on the table. Then I did an awkward run-walk to the elevator, where I hopped from one foot to the other until the final "ding" landed me on the main floor.

I burst through the front doors, throwing off my "Be quiet in the hospital" caution.

"Officer Snyder?!"

Through the windshield, I could see his blond head jerk up as he reached for his side. I ran around the car as he clambered out, whipping a probing gaze back through the hospital doors. When he realized there was no one following me, he squatted down and looked me in the eyes.

"What's up, Audrey?"

I launched into what I hoped was a rational-sounding story. I explained everything that Max and I knew again—the knife, barrel, and lock-pick set we'd found in the woods, the Khmer we'd heard spoken—and then I told him about the barrel that had fallen on Max. I knew I was probably repeating myself from my earlier report, but I honestly couldn't remember everything I'd told him, and I wanted these jerks found. I couldn't afford to forget anything. I stared at my tennis shoes as I dug a hole in the flowerbed.

"I'm going to call this in, Audrey. Wait here, okay?"

"Hi, officer. Do you want me to take Audrey back to the dive shop?"

It was Shawn's voice, but it didn't sound right. I turned and found him standing behind me. But what if Shawn was one of them?

I glanced back at what Shawn was seeing. Officer Snyder was talking quietly into the walkie-talkie on his shoulder.

"Um . . . yeah. Chief said that would be a good idea. He wants me to go check on something. Just be careful, Shawn." The way he said it, I knew the chief trusted Shawn. I took a deep breath. . . . Shawn wasn't involved.

Officer Snyder turned back to the radio as Shawn and I walked to Shawn's station wagon at the back of the parking lot.

He started the car and I leaned my forehead against the cool glass of the passenger window. I could almost imagine that none of this had happened.

"I just need to pick up a friend first, okay?"

I nodded in response, my eyes closed; I was barely awake.

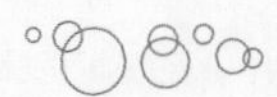

Strong arms lifted me from the car seat. I thought that it must have been my dad, until I realized that the shirt I was pressed against smelled of dirty sweat and smoke. My eyes snapped open a split second after I attempted my first swing. My arms were bound together and so were my legs. I was trapped.

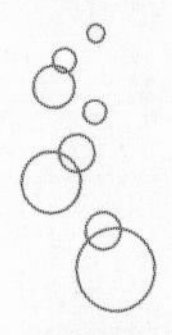

Chapter 16

"Stay still, Audrey. We don't want to hurt you." It was Shawn's voice—muffled, hard to hear. I swung my body, trying to find the voice, desperate for help. I had a close-up view of a dirty red flannel shirt, but couldn't see Shawn. The man carrying me had me slung across his shoulder, and Shawn must have been walking in front of him. I twisted and turned, looking for something to explain what was going on. None of the houses I could see looked occupied. No window blinds moved discreetly. There was no one around. Were we at the abandoned cottages?

"I didn't want to do this, Audrey, but you know way too much," said Shawn's voice. I was breathing hard, my stomach jammed against a powerful shoulder.

Maybe it was the lack of oxygen, but I couldn't think straight. What was Shawn doing? *Who* didn't want to hurt me? I knew too much about . . . what? Then it hit me—Shawn *was* one of them. I shook my head. Shawn would not do this.

The brute carrying me stopped in front of the door to a yellow-colored house; smudges of dirt and scuff marks from shoes were scattered liberally across the bottom of the door. I heard Shawn open the door and step inside; my captor followed.

The house was similar in layout to Max's house. Unlike the empty houses in the neighborhood, this one showed evidence of recent use, but the place hadn't been cleaned in weeks. The trash in the kitchen overflowed with Chinese take-out boxes.

They carried me into a back bedroom and dumped me on the floor. The impact hurt my backside, and I blinked back tears.

Shawn is one of them. My brain was starting to move. Slowly, but at least it was moving. Shawn was one of them, and he had just kidnapped me. He'd overheard me talking to the officer. He said that I knew too much. How did the cops not have any idea Shawn might be involved?

I flinched as Shawn stooped down toward me with a knife in his hand. Now I just wished my brain would *stop*.

He reached behind me and took my hands, which were bound behind my back. Relief coursed through me. He wasn't going to hurt me. He was going to cut the tape around my wrists. Maybe I would be okay after all.

"Leave her." The brute towered over Shawn. Shawn straightened abruptly, shaking his head. The bigger man leaned over to whisper into Shawn's ear, his clear blue eyes shifting toward me. I swallowed hard, silently cheering Shawn on as the man's paws clenched and unclenched.

I stared at the pair, unconsciously switching to investigator mode, cataloging the other man's appearance. Dark, greasy hair. Red-plaid flannel shirt and jeans that had a slightly brownish look to them. He put his hand on Shawn's shoulder. The hand was remarkably clean, his nails trimmed. Now, I realize that I get nosy at inconvenient times, but this was odd. I began to catalog again. A steady, confident stance. Bright white teeth. He wasn't drunk and didn't have the beer belly of the guys that made a habit of it.

At that moment he turned back to me, clenching his square, unshaven jaw. I dropped my eyes. Whoever he was, this man meant business. I had to get away. But, how? My hands and feet were tied and I didn't know for sure where I was.

After the pair left, I studied the room, looking for anything I could use to cut through the tape around my ankles and wrists. Bracing myself against the wall, I pushed up with my shoulder until I could get up on my knees; then I looked out the window.

Nothing but trees. No clues there.

I had to come up with a plan. Even if I managed to escape, I couldn't just run—okay, make that hobble and jump—away from the house. Shawn and his partner would find me in no time.

The voices in the other room were moving. "Just don't let her get out of here or it will blow everything."

"I know."

Shawn said good-bye and the door slammed shut. I slid back into a seated position as I heard footsteps coming toward my room.

Shawn cracked open the door and draped a blanket over me. "Sorry about this, kid. You won't need to stay here long. We're almost done. We have one more thing to finish and I'll get you out of here. Just stay out of the way." He was almost pleading with me. So I nodded, pretending both to understand and to agree with him. But when the door closed, I stuck my tongue out at him. The only act of defiance I could get away with.

I heard a cell phone ring, followed by Shawn's hushed voice—almost a whisper. "I know she just about blew everything, but she's out of the way now. Let's just get this thing finished." A pause. "If she disappears for long, the cops will be all over us. We need to go tonight." Another pause. "Give me five minutes."

He opened the door and poked his head in. "I'll be back later. Just stay quiet."

I started to plead with him. I'm hungry. I'm cold. Anything I could think of. I didn't want him leaving me in his hideout by myself. He was the only one who could protect me. Shawn just shook his head, leaned over, and put a strip of tape over my mouth, my tears wetting his hands. Then he left.

Dear God, please help me. It was all I could manage. But at this moment, I somehow knew that God could hear me despite everything I'd done in the last few days.

I was normally not a drippy, crying female, but I was scared, cold, and exhausted. I knew I needed to get out of this house, but I couldn't process anything. Curling up on the floor, I covered myself with the blanket the best I could, using my teeth, and tried to think.

Chapter 17

I don't remember ever falling asleep. But I remember waking. My joints were stiff. My shoulder ached from lying on the hard floor. And my eyes were gritty from tears mixed with dust and grime.

It was dark outside, and I was alone.

Moving slowly, I tried to stand. My efforts, more accurately described as hopeless flailing, resulted in just a few nasty bruises and my being out of breath. I rolled back onto my knees and forced myself to think. What in the room could I use to free myself? Unlike the kitchen, the room was absolutely empty. No trash. No bed. No chair. Just me and my now rather grubby shirt and shorts.

Lord, I need help. Please tell me what to do. Wait a minute. Me and my shorts with my *pocketknife* in them. Yep, I'm really good in a crisis.

After some more flailing around on the floor, I was able to retrieve my knife from my back pocket and open it. No easy feat. And it was an even better trick to saw through the tape around my wrists when I couldn't see a thing, but I only nicked myself once. The tape binding my legs was the next to go, then the strip across my mouth.

I stood up carefully and looked down at myself. There wasn't much light coming in the window, but I could see well enough to know my mom was going to kill me. I really did look like something they deposited on the lakeshore.

Going out the window did not look like fun—it would be a nasty drop—and since I was alone, I thought I'd try the door first. I tiptoed to the door and tried the knob. The door was unlocked. I swallowed hard and pulled the door open a crack. The brute was sitting at the kitchen table, facing me. His dog—Jaws—was sprawled on the floor at his feet. Fortunately, the guy had his nose stuck in a book and his maroon cap was pulled down, covering much of his upper face. Even with him distracted and his vision somewhat blocked, there was no way I was going out there with him. I pulled the door shut.

I turned toward the window and took a deep breath. I guess I'd just drop and roll. If the guys on TV could do it without killing themselves, I could do it, too, right?

As I reached to unlock the window, a pair of headlight beams swept across the woods and then stopped just inches from my window. I jerked my head back to avoid being illuminated by the lights of what appeared to be a red sports car. I could hear my heart thudding and my hands were shaking. Mr. Broome?

The front door opened and closed.

"How's she doing?" It was Shawn. A chair scraped against the floor and I heard footsteps coming toward my door. I scrambled, picking up the tape and flinging myself to the floor. I yanked the blanket back over myself and prayed.

"Haven't heard a peep. I checked on her not too long ago and she was sound asleep."

"I won't bother her then." The footsteps moved away from the bedroom door. The front door opened and closed again, bringing more voices and the faint smell of pizza. My stomach growled.

"You do *not* want pizza from them," I whispered to my belly as I returned to the window and flicked the slide lock to open it. But the window wouldn't budge. I squinted at the window. It looked like it might have been painted shut. I pulled out my knife and started scraping at the paint, desperate to get the window open.

I don't know how long I'd been at it when my hand slipped and hit the window with a thud, and the voices stopped. I wiped my hands on my jeans and listened for footsteps.

"Yeah, well, you guys haven't seen anything yet." I released the breath I'd been holding and turned to go back to scraping. "The money we made this time is chump change," the third voice continued.

I stopped again and listened to the voice rant about how they'd fooled the cops by stashing the loot in barrels they'd dropped into the lake. I whipped back to the window—I was done for. Shawn would tell them I knew and that'd be it.

"Yeah, it's a good thing no one knows about that." It was the flannel-shirted brute that had been with Shawn. Was he protecting me? Why didn't he tell the rest of them that I knew what was going on?

I was so dumbfounded with the brute brushing my knowledge off that I almost missed the fourth voice. "Well, you two have done a good job. I'd say I trust you to move on to some bigger things now." I recognized this voice; I just couldn't quite place it. I willed him to speak more so that I could connect his voice with a face, but the other guys joined in, talking and planning.

I went back to the window and pulled again. It moved a fraction. I was getting somewhere.

Spreading my feet, I bent my knees and pushed hard from underneath. Finally, the window flew open. I stuck my head out and contemplated how to jump out of a two-story window without killing myself.

I swallowed and started to swing my feet over the sill, but stopped cold. There was another car pulling up. When they climbed out of the car, I could see that these guys were armed. With one foot out the window, I didn't move for fear of drawing their attention and being seen. When they disappeared around the side of the house, I dropped my other foot out the window, turned to hold onto the sill, and let my body swing down. I held on to the sill for a moment, taking deep breaths. Then I let go and hit the ground with a sickening crunch.

I had planned to reach the ground and roll, but I'd hit the ground quicker than I'd expected. I was breathing hard, and tears were squeezing out my eyes. My left ankle was on fire with pain.

I gritted my teeth and rolled over onto my stomach. I had to keep moving. If I could reach the street, maybe I'd find that one of the jerks inside the house had left their keys in their car. I started with a crawling slither thing without getting very far, so I pushed myself up onto one foot and began hopping.

I'd gone about three steps when I heard a bunch of shouting and a splintering crash followed by the crack of gunfire. They were firing at me!

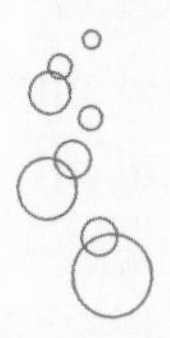

Chapter 18

I dropped back to the ground and, ignoring the pain, began slithering to the edge of the woods for protection. The gunshots should bring the police. Now I just had to survive long enough for them to arrive.

I hadn't yet reached the woods when I saw the telltale swirling lights turn a corner. Then they were here. The red strobe light cast an odd shadow across the grass to the place where I lay. At any other time I might have found the flashing lights disturbing, but at this moment, I was just grateful for whatever safety they might bring.

The muffled sounds of shouts and searches continued in the house as I pushed myself back up to my feet, shifting nearly all of my weight to one leg.

A police search light swept across the grass and stopped on me. Good. Now I could wait for them to come get me.

"Hey, there's another one. Grab her!" It took a moment for it to register that they were talking about me. I saw the shadow of a rather large-looking gun come up around the car in front of me. I threw my hands up automatically. That's what you're supposed to do, I hoped.

"Lie down on the ground." The serious voice echoed around among the houses. I cringed at the pain as I obeyed.

An officer cautiously moved out from the car and walked toward me, his gun trained on me. As he approached me, I tried to find my voice, but I was sobbing and my tongue was glued to the back of my throat. The only sound I could make slip through my throat was a strangled, "Ah . . . ah . . ."

The officer put his gun into his holster, pulled out his handcuffs, and threw them around my wrists. He pulled me up, but I collapsed back to the ground.

"Stand up," he commanded.

"I can't." I rolled to a sitting position. As he reached down to grab me again, I heard Shawn's voice say, "Officer, she's one of the good guys. That's the Barringer kid."

Shawn was standing at the top of the hill with his flannel shirt-wearing buddy. I knew they were probably standing still, but they appeared to be slowly swaying in circles. I sat still while the officer removed the handcuffs. I should have been annoyed with the "kid" remark, but I was having trouble digging up the irritation.

"Are you okay?" The officer's face was dark in the shadows, but I could hear the concern in his voice.

I didn't know what to do or think, but my anger suddenly won over the other emotions I'd been dealing with.

"What in the world is going on?" I didn't know *who* I was demanding information from, but someone had better help me figure things out. I stood gingerly, shaking. I looked toward the police officer. "These jerks kidnapped me." I turned on Shawn, "You grabbed me from the hospital and now you're parading around here acting like, 'Hey, I'm Mr. Good Guy'? I don't think so." I turned and pointed at the brute. "And that guy tied me up and stood watch while Shawn went off and did heaven knows what. Officer, you need to arrest them."

The officer looked questioningly at Shawn.

"Aud, I'm sorry I scared you. When I heard everything you'd found, I knew you wouldn't be safe at the hospital. My dad and his girlfriend were going to be coming to the hospital to visit Max. She already suspected you guys knew something. And if she'd found out what you knew before *I* did . . ." Shawn looked away and watched the officers put a red-nosed woman into the car—and that's when it clicked. Familiar Voice wasn't a guy. It was Janine—the girlfriend and former suspected accomplice in art theft—with a cold.

The officer put his hand on my shoulder. "Are you okay?"

I just shook my head.

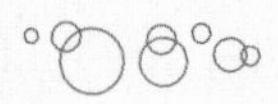

The next thing I remember was opening my eyes and looking up at a white shiny ceiling with red flashing lights. It took me a moment to realize that I was in an ambulance. The machines were beeping all around me, and I closed my eyes, grateful to be where I was. *Thank you, Lord. We're all safe.*

Chapter 19

The doctors said I was fortunate not to have broken my ankle. A "moderate ankle sprain and a hairline fracture in the big toe" didn't seem to cover the pain shooting up my lower leg, but the doctor had been sure. She just shook her head and said, "Keep it wrapped and stay off of it for at least two weeks."

She had given my mom a prescription for the swelling and one to help me sleep if I needed it. I didn't. My head hit my pillow, and I was out.

For the next five days I hid in my room. My head, ankle, and about every inch of my body in between, hurt. I let my mom pamper me for once, but none of her care helped what really hurt deep down.

I talked to Max on the phone several times a day. He seemed to be doing okay. The doctors told him his leg was healing fine. I could hear in his voice that he was tired and not sleeping well, but I didn't expect much more. Through association with a criminal, Max's family was being grilled about a string of nasty burglaries and, to top it off, his best friend had nearly gotten him killed trying to solve the mystery.

Mrs. Myer had decided not to continue working on the story for the newspaper due to her personal interest in the case. Another reporter, who wasn't nearly as creative as Mrs. Myer, finished the piece, and follow-up articles, for the press.

I forced myself to read the depressing reports. Janine had posed as a maid for hire, an interior designer, or a worker for any other respectable profession, to gain access to the wealthy homes around the lake. She'd case a place, study and photograph the artwork, and then somehow make good forgeries. Then the crew would boat in, switch the paintings, steal some other expensive items while they were at it, and then take off, dropping the artwork in sealed barrels for later retrieval.

One of Janine's major mistakes had been borrowing Mr. Broome's car while he was out of the country. While she had permission to use the car, it was just too "one of a kind" to park around the city without drawing attention . . . especially since everyone knew Mr. Broome was gone. A police friend from Mr. Broome's years in court got curious when it kept showing up near the dive shop and the abandoned cottages. She started following Janine around here and there, eventually putting two and two together.

No one knew why Janine had hidden the real focus of the burglaries. But everyone suspected that since she'd been accused of art theft before, Janine would have been an obvious suspect if the police had realized that the art was the main target. From how she treated Max's dad after she was arrested, it certainly wasn't out of a desire to protect Mr. Myer.

I still hadn't figured out exactly how Shawn was involved, though, and I certainly wasn't going to ask Max about it. My folks weren't talking directly to me about it, either. But it was obvious that Shawn had found out what his dad's girlfriend was up to and had ended up being an informant for the police . . . probably to help prove his dad wasn't involved. I couldn't imagine how hard it had been for him. It was no wonder he'd been unbearable the last few months.

But it was Max I thought about most. After saying I was sorry about a million times, I had no idea what to say to cheer Max up. So I avoided the topic of his dad, his dad's relationship with Janine, the burglaries, and the accident. I knew it wasn't the best idea, but I couldn't think of another option. I couldn't exactly pray. I had a feeling that I'd used up all the favors reserved for a horrible failure of a Christian.

On Sunday, my dad talked my mom into taking me to church, saying it would be good for me to get out. I wasn't sure I wanted to face God again this soon after everything that had happened, but I was still trying to be my new self. So I just obeyed.

The singing was wonderful, but the words from last week still rattled in my brain. I knew God still hated me for what I'd done.

Pastor James prayed and everyone got up to leave. I'd missed another sermon. I picked up my crutches and started making my way to my class. Without thinking, I wove my way through the crowd. At the last moment, I turned to go outside instead of to my class—I just couldn't face the kids or the leaders.

I swung my way toward a rock under one of the trees out back and managed to sit somewhat gracefully . . . at least I didn't end up in a heap on the ground.

"Audrey?" It was Pastor James. Pastors had that special talent for seeing right through people. He was the last person I wanted to face right now.

"Audrey, would you mind if I sat with you?" What could I say, *no*? I just nodded and he sat next to me, his forehead wrinkled up as he looked at me.

"You've been through a lot, huh?" I know he was trying to be nice, but I couldn't look him in the eyes. Instead, I examined my slightly dusty shoes.

He put his arm around me and squeezed. "I'm so proud of you, Audrey." *Proud? Proud!*

"How can you be proud?" The words sounded harsh, even to me.

He just nodded. I had to fill the silence.

"I lied. I disobeyed my parents. I nearly got my best friend killed. And you're proud?" I was on a roll now. "What happened to, 'The LORD detests lying lips'? What happened to, 'You messed up'? What happened to . . . to, 'Audrey, you're an awful person who's constantly getting into trouble'? How can you be proud of that?"

I hated him for getting me to say it out loud. I had tried to push it down, make it go away. But he had ripped away what little protection I'd made for myself and had made me look at how ugly I really was.

"Yeah. You messed up, all right." And that was supposed to make me feel better?

"Audrey, I think you've missed the point of God—and church too, for that matter." Really, with all the obey-your-parents reminders, I don't think I could have missed it. A reply was forming, but Pastor James stopped me by calmly taking my chin in his hand and forcing me to look into his gray eyes. He was smiling so big, every single tooth in his mouth showed. I couldn't help being curious.

"Will you read something for me?" he asked, his eyes drilling into mine. I dropped my eyes and barely nodded. "Look up Romans 5:8 before you get too down on yourself." He gave me one more squeeze and stood up. I watched him push through the glass door and walk back inside.

I stared at the door, blinking until long after his dark coat and graying head had disappeared. My gaze dropped to the Bible I had dropped by the rock. I swallowed, afraid of what I'd find. But I'd promised and didn't want to risk lying again. Picking up the Bible, I flipped to the passage and read, "But God demonstrates his own love for us in this: While we were still sinners, Christ died for us."

I took a breath and blinked. God loved me even though I had messed up. *Lord, I am really sorry for everything I've done this past week.* I wasn't going to get all gushy, but I didn't know how else to say thanks to him for forgiving me for my string of rather large mess-ups. I squinted, looking up at the bright white clouds floating in the sky, and sighed.

I was saved another bout of tears by my little sister running up the sidewalk, golden curls flying, just to give me a hug. I guess she wasn't such a pain after all.

"Mom said we could go to the hospital and check on Max." It was the best idea I'd heard all week. I stood up, and she handed me my crutches.

"Thanks." I grinned at her as she raced to the car.

I was already starting to feel better.

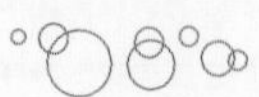

At the hospital, we found Max sitting up with his mom and Shawn, watching a preacher on television. He turned and grinned at me before he clicked it off. My folks shook hands with Mrs. Myer. "Mrs. Myer, Shawn. Let us get you two some coffee." Mrs. Myer nodded. Shawn hefted up Suzie, and they left so Max and I could talk. The problem was, I didn't know what to say.

I sat in the armchair Mrs. Myer had vacated. Max was still hooked up to some of the machines, and I couldn't take my eyes off them.

"So, we both survived," he said, smiling at me.

"No thanks to me." I was feeling guilty again.

"It wasn't just your fault, Audrey. I disobeyed my mom, too."

"It was my idea though." He couldn't argue with that.

He looked at me, his jaw clenching. Then he spit into his hand

and reached out for mine. Now, I'm not a sissy girl, but spit-swearing was still disgusting.

"I'll swear not to disobey if you do the same." Great. Someone to make sure I stayed on the straight-and-narrow. Just what I needed. I wrinkled my nose, spit into my hand, and shook his.